BAG O' GOODIES

Jolly Walker Bittick

FIRST EDITION
www.jollywalkerbittick.com

ISBN: 978-1-7370309-4-2

To voluptuous variety:

the spice of life

TABLE OF CONTENTS

Cherry Popped Book

Well damn
All that it took
A life free of alcohol and women, bam
A cherry popped book

This one is unique and special
This one has obliqueness tinted consequential
The pages look normal
The line here you are reading will not rhyme

Enjoy this ride, the book and literary glide
I see it as a jive
The written word is well and alive
Fun in reading and writing is something I like to abide

By

Seemed like a word best left alone
Just like this book, volume one
Named that after the sequel is released
My impatience appeased
I'm hopeful the readers are acquiesced

That word, I always wanted to use
I did! Look
Enjoy this at your own risk
A cherry popped book

Calvert County Detention

It was a hot and humid Tuesday. After returning home from work and changing into more casual clothing, I cleaned up, washed the dishes, and mowed the front lawn. Once finished, I made the fateful decision to treat myself to some libations at a local bar.

As somewhat of a regular, I received a complimentary beer from the bartender, Melinda, who often gave me special attention in exchange for my generous tips. Boilermakers were often my drink of choice, and on that Tuesday, I began my evening of drinking well before sundown when the older folks were inhabiting the joint. The vibe was good enough that a few boilermakers too many seemed inevitable.

In the beginning, old Ned, Tommy J., LaWanda, and Gale Proskey, a Navy vet, sat in the nicely air conditioned bar. Outside was a tiki bar, which at first was empty. It was often better suited for the evenings to avoid the worst of the grueling summer heat. I opted to sit next to old Ned. Wearing a full head of white hair that draped beyond his shoulders, and sporting a long unkept beard that was equal in color, he raised his bottle of beer.

"Evenin," he greeted.

I raised mine and took a sip.

3

"Do young men work anymore?"

I smiled. "It's called nine to five."

He ran his hand down his beard. "I did that for awhile."

LaWanda, big and boisterous with plump cheeks on her face as well as down below, leaned into the bar to face Ned from beyond Tommy J.

"Did what? Work 'nine to five' or drink instead?" she asked.

The two began a drunken, heated exchange. Tommy J. leaned back and grinned as Gale Proskey faced upward at the Keno screen playing in the corner.

"Ready for another hun?" Melinda asked.

I reacted with a smile and slid my shot glass to her. She was a taller-than-average woman and looked to be around my age. She was married with three kids, but patrons young and old marveled at her still-good looks.

"You're psychic, huh?" I asked.

She gave a smirk and poured the whiskey. "No hun, I just know my alcoholics well."

I nodded as she replaced the shot. After slinging it back and giving a wince, I sipped my beer to chase it.

"Don't you have anything better to do?" she continued.

"I'm bored. Chores are done at the house."

"You know you're good looking, right?" she replied.

"So are you."

She raised her hand showing the nice rock on her ring finger.

"Doesn't mean I can't be truthful."

Melinda gave an appreciative smile before returning to serve the others. Gale Proskey slammed his hands on the bar.

"Them terrible numbers! I tell you, that game is rigged," he snapped.

Gale Proskey had been a Gunners Mate Second Class on the USS Constellation during the Vietnam War. He always wore a vintage (and sweat drenched) Navy ball cap with applicable insignia. I tried my best to avoid him at times because he was prone to lecture the hell out of anyone within range about the military and the current state of the world. Unfortunately, he noticed me beyond the chatter from old Ned and LaWanda, and the silent Tommy J. Once over his loss in Keno, and provided with a new beer, he fixated on me and approached.

"I'll say! How's your evening young man?" he greeted.

I smiled for posterity. "Oh, you know, just another Tuesday evening."

He patted my back. "We talked before, right?"

In fact, we seemed to talk every time we saw each other.

"I think so. You're an old Gunners Mate from the Constellation, correct?"

His smile broadened. "Yes, and you were in as well, weren't ya?"

5

"I worked on helicopters."

Gale Proskey put his hand around me and began a lecture. Something kept me from being rude and pushing him off or weaseling out of the unwanted chatter. I suppose it was my respect for the elderly and fellow veterans. My head bobbed slowly as I maintained a smirking smile to give the guise of interest. Melissa's resupplying of my drinks was enough to give me the necessary buzz. Luckily, Tommy J. came to my rescue when he called for Gale Proskey to take his seat for another round of Keno, which seemed to be the one thing he found more important than lecturing the rest of us. As he returned to his stool, I motioned for Melinda to get Tommy J. a drink on me.

The sun had gone down and more people arrived at the bar. The younger crowd filled in and with them were the gorgeous women wearing summer attire generous to a man's eyes. They proceeded to the tiki bar outside. As there seemed to be an unusually high number of patrons at the establishment for a Tuesday, I asked about the occasion. Melinda indicated that a cornhole league began convening at the bar on Tuesdays. My constant glaring at the beauties outside prompted her to nudge me. I took the hint and grabbed my drinks.

As the air was thick and humid with a southern scent, the chatter from the large group drowned out the sound of the cicadas in the distance. Seated at the edge of the bar closest to the

6

cornhole groups, I surveilled the crowd for the women that motivated me to relocate. Country music blared from the jukebox as some of the bystanders danced. My eyes connected with another's—a dirty blonde wearing a tight orange top and cutoff jean shorts. It was hard to make out her eye color, but her smile in my direction was enough to steal my attention. A hand grabbing my left arm distracted me.

"Here," Melinda said as she handed me a beer. "This one's on me. Go talk to them!"

I gave her a thankful nod before taking the beer and proceeding towards the dirty blonde; her smile grew.

"Hi," I started.

She responded in kind.

"Are you in the cornhole leagues?"

She shook her head. "My sister and her husband are. I'm Eva."

I introduced myself and we took a seat at a picnic table facing the games. We talked. After awhile, Eva's sister and husband introduced themselves while also introducing me to whatever jello shots they were having. Three or four shots in, and Eva's breasts seemed particularly large, her eyes more succulent, and her lips kiss-ready. I leaned in. She pushed against my chest.

"Wait."

I sat back and smirked.

"You're really cute," she continued. "Tell you what…"

She retrieved a pen and crumpled receipt from her purse, writing on the back of it.

"My number. I just don't want to do anything here."

I nodded. "I see."

I was well into my buzz and could not help but check her out. At some point, her sister approached and told me to meet them at another bar in neighboring Calvert County. My drunkenness did not seem to disturb them, and I entered the address of the location in my phone. The cornhole games were wrapping up. Eva told me to meet them at the other place shortly. I took her cue and made a stop at the bathroom before leaving.

Once in my pickup, a white 2020 Chevrolet Silverado, I entered the address into the dash GPS. The destination was sixteen miles away. Feeling hungry, I stopped at a convenience store two stoplights down and bought a made to order panini. Without bothering to recall what toppings I requested, I paid for the meal and returned to my truck. I paid little attention to how much of the panini made it into my mouth as I drove. Warm spots on my thighs indicated that some of it failed to make it to the intended destination. Tossing the paper wrapping onto the passenger seat, I dozed into a comfortable state imagining Eva at the next bar. The thought of the many possibilities that the night was sure to behold proved invigorating.

A thump and the sight of railings to the left and right glaring from the pickup's high beams revealed the Benedict Bridge. I was crossing the Patuxent River. In the moment, it seemed fine that the double yellow lines ran directly under my pickup rather than to the left. Feeling well fed and thinking about what I was going to do once I got to my destination, I entered Calvert County on the other side of the bridge. Humming to the tune playing on the radio, a parked car appeared on the right shoulder just before a gravel parking area to a liquor store and truck rental shop. As the vehicle appeared in the rearview mirror further and further back, its headlights came on. It pulled onto the roadway. Blue flashing lights gave away its identity.

"Fuck."

The vehicle sped up and was close behind. I looked on to ensure I was in the proper lane before pulling to the shoulder. From the driver's side of the vehicle, a spotlight glared towards me overshining the blue lights.

"Sorry Eva," I said, looking into the rearview mirror.

The driver's door opened on the vehicle. A figure holding a flashlight walked towards me; only feet were visible under the bobbing light. I rolled down the window.

"Hello. How are we doing tonight?" the officer greeted.

I tried looking at his name tag to see if I could read it in the limited light. I could not.

"I was doing pretty good."

"Can I see your license, registration, and insurance?"

I sarcastically smiled as I got them. The situation was simple; my chances of avoiding jail were slim.

"Do you know why I pulled you over?"

"Actually, no."

"Have you had anything to drink tonight, sir?"

I nodded. "Had a few."

He flashed his light at my license. "Interesting name."

"Thanks."

I still could not make out his name, but then he handed my materials back to me.

"Sir, can I have you step out of the vehicle and perform a field sobriety test? Be advised that you are on camera."

My legal mind told me to say 'no', but my macho side told me that I could pull off the test and be on my way to see Eva and company.

"Sure can."

I no sooner opened the pickup door and took a step out when I stumbled forward and the officer grabbed my upper arm to keep me upright.

"Well, shit."

"Sir, go ahead and follow my light forward putting one foot in front of the other, toe to heal."

Three steps into the test and I stumbled, again. Things did not look good.

"Keep going, all the way to my light shining on the ground."

Two more steps and I wobbled, but this time I continued.

"Okay, sir, do you consent to a field blood alcohol content test?"

Finally, my legal wit kicked in.

"I'm good."

He shook his head. "I can't have you drive in this condition."

I looked at him, this time I could see the name "Dottinger" on his name plate. "You're just doing your job. I get it."

"I appreciate that," he replied.

Officer Dottinger placed me under arrest providing me with my Miranda Rights. Cuffed, and being walked to his police vehicle, I asked him about where my truck would be taken. Ironically, the backup officer that arrived during the stop indicated that my truck would simply be parked in the liquor store parking lot at the scene. I laughed, Officer Dottinger followed suit. He then placed me in the back seat of the cruiser as we left.

"So, why are you out in this condition tonight?"

I stared out the window at the cornfields visible under the moonlight.

"Nothing better to do," I replied.

"You seem like a nice guy."

"Thanks."

He looked at me through the rearview mirror, which was hard to notice through the barrier separating the back seats from the front.

"Are you military?"

"I'm a veteran."

"Thank you for your service," he replied.

"You're welcome."

Officer Dottinger explained that I would be taken to a holding cell and provided information on the state's policies towards BAC testing refusals. I knew my license was likely to be toast as a result of the night's unfortunate turn, but in the moment I was more interested in sleep. The drive seemed long, and after the small talk in the beginning, the rest of the ride was solemn. There was little anger in my mind about what happened; I did not feel sorry for myself so much as I was unhappy that my plans were foiled by a car parked on a shoulder that forced me to react.

After a short ride down a narrow, darkened road, we arrived at an undisclosed location. A large light shining down revealed a brick building featuring a large steel door. The parking lot appeared empty, and the building looked more like a utility structure than something associated with law enforcement.

"Nice building," I said.

Officer Dottinger looked at me through the rearview mirror.

"The holding cell?" I continued.

"Yep. It's a rural county. This is what they give us."

"I guess I'm lucky."

He faced me. "I'm sorry?"

"I'm the only one here tonight."

"Oh, no. You will be here for a bit. I'll be taking you to the jail afterwards."

I tried to look at it as a good thing, but nothing about the night was good. Officer Dottinger helped me out of the car, cuffed. We proceeded down a ramp through the single lit steel doorway. As the door clanged shut behind us, we proceeded down the long white hallway to a single-windowed door on the left. Another officer filled out paperwork at a table on the right side facing a brick wall. After nodding at Officer Dottinger and glancing at me, he returned to writing. I was walked to a seat in the corner.

"Okay, do you agree to submit to an official Blood Alcohol Content test?" Dotting asked.

A split second was all I needed to make a legal decision, to which I shook my head.

"Sir, please sign this," the other officer said, handing me a green document.

After a moment, Dottinger took it from my hand.

"If you want to be able to get your truck once we release you, sign it," he said.

I nodded, then retrieved the document to provide my signature.

"In lieu of your test refusal, you will be granted fourteen days to drive before which time you will have to appeal the suspension, or have your license revoked," the other officer explained.

Dottinger handed the signed document to him. I tried checking his nameplate, but I never saw it. Tired, I began to nod off.

"Where exactly were you off to?" the officer asked.

"To meet up with some girls."

Dottinger held back laughter. "They might be disappointed tonight."

"I'm sure they will be," I replied.

The two chuckled, then Dottinger walked me to a holding cell across the corridor. He indicated that I would be held there until they were done processing their paperwork, then I was to be taken to the jail. The holding cell was barren with a toilet, fountain, and concrete slab to rest on. The concrete was predictably cold and not particularly comfortable to rest on. Desperate to get a nap in, I rolled my blue polo as best I could into a makeshift pillow to give my head and neck some relief. Unfortunately, my naked upper body—tattoos and all—was exposed to the cold, miserable surface.

"Alright," a voice called.

I opened my eyes, realizing I had napped after all.

"Let's get you to the jail," Dottinger said.

My polo was disheveled, but I hastily put it on before approaching the bars. Dottinger slid the door open and nodded towards the hallway exit.

"Have you been to jail before?" he asked.

Groggy, I cleared my throat before responding, "Yes."

"You seem pretty square, I guess everybody has their moments, huh."

"Looks can be deceiving."

"That's a fact," he responded.

After seating me in the back of the cruiser, cuffed, he radioed in of our impending arrival to the jail. We then departed. I rested my head and tried to sneak in another nap on the last stretch of the ride, but Dottinger was apparently bored.

"So where are you from?"

I slowly lifted my head. "Out west. Been on the east coast for a while though."

"I see. Well, we should have you up and on your way sometime later today."

"Cool."

I saw a row of lights approaching on the right side, then a large fence. We arrived at the jail. Dottinger drove around the back to an entryway similar to the one at the holding facility.

"Isn't this where we just were?" I joked.

Dottinger peered through the rearview mirror. "Nah."

He stopped the car, announced our arrival via radio, then got me out of the back seat. We proceeded through the bulky door into a corridor, then to the control room. Calvert County was rural enough to do the intake in the same space as the cell control room was located, something I found to be interesting. I posed for the customary booking photo, then the officers issued me a jumpsuit with slippers. They motioned to a door across from the front counter which was a restroom where I changed. The officers on duty at the jail were less talkative than Dottinger, who nodded to me before leaving. I knew things were going to be boring for a bit. After confiscating my clothes and putting them into a bag with the rest of my items, I was walked to cell "3" and uncuffed. The haze grey walls and matching bunks did little to inspire. There was no way that I could be released fast enough.

After the clanging of the cell door being slid shut, I glanced at the four bunks in the cell. All empty, with scant mattresses and scantier blankets. Though not a common visitor to jail cells, I saw this one (the jail as a whole) as being unique with bunks and blankets. My previous stint in a cell involved a room full of other men and nothing more than concrete to rest upon. I smirked, then tossed myself onto the bottom bunk closet to me, on the left. Eyes closed and body relaxed, I zoned into my thoughts and tried to use the image of Eva in my mind to get me through my stay. Her fluttering hair, glowing smile, and generous features had me smiling in my thoughts. She was telling me it was "okay", that we would reconnect sometime in the future maybe. Everything was fine it seemed.

"Breakfast or not?" a voice called out.

I opened my eyes and rubbed them. Standing at the foot of the bunk was a heavyset officer with coke bottle glasses holding a tray of food. I sat up; it neither looked nor smelled appetizing.

"No, I'm good. Thanks," I said.

The officer slowly shook his head before exiting the cell. As the door clanged shut again, I tried returning to the dream state. My eyes seemed more focused on the inside of my eyelids than on pretty women, and after some time I was startled by the doors opening and a commotion.

"Dog, I heard you. I'm going," a voice said.

"Last warning. You're already on thin ice," another snapped.

I looked at the door, now open, and in came two men escorted by an officer with another behind him.

"There's nothing to discuss," the second officer replied, "you will be here until the Commissioner can see you."

The second man shook his head. "This 'som bullshit. For real."

The officers stood in the doorway as the two men took the lower bunks on adjacent units. I rubbed my eyes again to get a better look at the scene, but the men were now silent, and the officers slowly exited before clanging the door shut, again.

"Deanna better not say shit. This whole thing is a joke," the first man said.

He was tall and slender with an afro and tattoo on his neck. In my mind I named him "Tall." His companion was much shorter and had corn rows. "Shorty" was the name I gave him. Neither seemed drunk.

"She won't. I bet that clerk threw shade on us," Shorty said.

The two laid on the bottom bunks facing upward. I rolled over to face the wall and try getting more sleep. After some time, I woke to the two fellas talking again. Light beamed through the lone window in the cell indicating that daylight arrived. I coughed, then sat up.

"Yo," Tall said.

I looked at him. "What's up?"

"How long do they hold people here?"

"I don't know. Never been here before."

Shorty shook his head as he continued facing upward. "Man, we be sittin here for a minute either way. We're in bum fuck."

"Yea," I said, "this is a different kind of set up. Rural county for sure."

Tall scoffed. "Thought you said you never been here."

"I haven't," I replied.

"He's talking about jail. You been in before?"

"Yea, years ago. On the Virginia side."

"They don't mess around over in V-A," Tall added.

I chuckled. "Apparently not here either."

18

"So, what did your cracka ass do?" Shorty asked.

"Got drunk, met a girl. Was going to meet her after hours, but Calvert County happened."

"Cock blocked," Tall replied.

"Yea. No point whining about it now. What about you guys?"

"Selling some shit. But bruhs know better than foolin around in these parts," Shorty replied.

"Where you coming from?"

Tall shook his head. "DC."

"Damn. Yea, that's tough."

"Who you tellin?" Shorty replied.

I almost felt bad for the two. Selling contraband that was interstate in nature had to come with much harsher penalties than what I was facing. They chatted amongst themselves. My eyelids grew heavy again; I turned over and tried getting some more sleep. Relaxation seemed fleeting, but the sound of the cell door opening again woke me. An officer had arrived with lunch. Tall and Shorty shook their heads, but I accepted mine. The shoddy ham sandwich and the apple slices were better than whatever was offered for breakfast. The 2% milk that accompanied the meal helped revive memories of the lunches at school in the forgettable cafeteria, and for a brief time, I felt mildly satisfied as I lay on the meager bunk. Another unknown quantity of time passed before the next noise disturbed me, this time it was Shorty banging on the cell door hoping to make a phone call. I sat up.

"Yo, officers, do we get a phone call or what?" he asked.

"That door is loud even when it's closed!" I said.

Tall chuckled. "DeSean, it's cool. Chill."

DeSean shook his head as he continued banging on the door.

"Cut it out!" a voice barked from beyond the door.

"What about a phone call, or are we leaving soon?" Desean replied.

"Bruh, don't push it," Tall said under his breath.

"You aren't going anywhere until you talk to the Commissioner," the voice answered.

"Who the hell is the Commissioner?" I mumbled.

Tall shrugged his shoulders as DeSean returned to his bunk.

"I guess in Maryland that's what they call the Magistrate," I continued.

"What did you do last time?" Tall asked.

I tilted my head and smirked.

"Dog, you like to get busted having a good time huh," he laughed.

I scratched my cheek and grinned. DeSean mumbled to himself from the bunk, then he and Tall began talking again. My eyes slowly closed, and more time passed. The angle of the light shining into the cell began to shift; I became aware once it started to beam onto my face from the window. Unable to rest any longer, I repositioned myself on the mattress and relaxed while staring at the bottom of the top bunk. Finally, the door clanged open and an officer entered.

"Come with me," he said pointing at me. I rose to my feet and the officer cuffed me. We proceeded to exit.

"Hopefully that means they'll call us soon," DeSean said.

The door clanged shut behind the officer and I, then at the control room counter he chained my feet. I trudged behind the officer as he escorted me through an adjacent passageway, through a hatchlike door, and into an unassuming room. The officer motioned for me to take a seat in an arm desk. After placing some paperwork on the desk, the officer turned on a large monitor mounted on the wall in front of me. The Commissioner appeared on the screen. As I had suspected, they were the equivalent to the Magistrate in Virginia. After issuing me the charges and penalties and giving me a "release on recognizance", I signed the paperwork. The officer turned the monitor off and escorted me, papers in hand, towards the control room. At the counter, the officers retrieved the bag with my clothing and items in it, then allowed me back into the restroom to change. After changing and signing a few additional documents at the counter, I was released.

Once outside of the Detention Center, I stood at the front entrance where a wide set of steps led down to the parking lot. I checked my phone. It was 4:30 in the afternoon. The battery was almost dead and I had nobody to call for a ride. The GPS map indicated that the trek to my truck involved a six mile hike. Pacing quickly across the parking lot to the county road, I realized that I missed an entire day's work without being able to call out. Cell service wasn't particularly good where I was, but it was enough to leave my supervisor a voice message explaining my no-call/no-show to work. From there, it was a long walk to the truck.

The Detention Center was tucked away in a wooded area at the end of a country road that meandered through ravines and was surrounded by spacious residential lots. The air was thick and humid as it had been the day before while my mind and body were numb. I had yet to mentally digest all that had occurred over the past 24 hours. A mile and a half walk down the road led to the intersection with the state route leading to the truck. I turned right and walked along its spacious shoulder. "Maryland 231", as a sign indicated, was a mostly straight road with only one major slope that gave way to the Patuxent River flood plain. The GPS map showed the sloped portion of the state route being the half-way point of the walk. Modest traffic gusted by in both directions.

With the ordeal of the previous night behind me, I checked my phone to see if Eva contacted me. Aside from my jail cell day-dreaming, she slipped my mind. There were no texts or missed calls, but I still could not help but grin. Eva was a fling that did not pan out because I got busted on the road. She understood that as well as me even if she did not know what actually happened. There were a million other things I could have done the night before. The costs from the pending DWI were going to be painful. In the end, I had no regrets. Living a loner's life came at a cost. For me, that cost was going to the bar and getting liquored up.

Besides a truck full of punks howling and squawking at me as they passed by, the six-plus mile walk was refreshing. The thick humidity left me soaked in sweat but also feeling good. Walking eastbound with traffic meant that the truck was going to be on the other side of the road. As I approached my destination, crab grass and tall brush obstructed my ability to see the liquor store or my pickup. The store finally appeared in the distance from a veering turn. A few hundred yards past more shrubs gave way to the sight of my truck in the dirt lot to the left of the store. My face lit up. *I'm back,* I thought to myself.

A row of trucks passed by going the other direction before it was clear to cross the road. I laughed at the sight of the liquor store and its bright "OPEN" sign atop the doorway. With irony, I had an appreciation for being arrested for DWI and then retrieving my truck at the site of a liquor store. To be sure nothing else happened, I rounded the truck to check for any damages. My memory seemed well intact from the night before, but I wanted to be certain. I opened the driver's side door and winced at the heat inside the cab. The center console was made of a black synthetic material which was scorching hot after sitting all day in the summer heat. After turning it on, I immediately put the air conditioner on blast. I was off.

Once on the highway, I proceeded across the Benedict Bridge, leaving Calvert County. Laughter was all I could muster when thinking of the night before. Though Eva was a hottie, I could not come to my senses about contacting her seeing as she had not contacted me. The night was a failure to the point that it seemed best to wipe clean all memories associated with the matter, women included. The remainder of the drive home was quiet with only the radio playing at low volume. I marveled at the unique green color of the Maryland summer foliage and relaxed into an odd sort of oblivion. The mess I got myself into was such that it simply was not worth dwelling on that day. A day off from any more worry seemed appropriate for the legal and financial troubles I was soon to be in.

Off the highway and on the winding backroads, I approached the Boundary Creek Subdivision where I lived. I turned left onto Creekside Drive and proceeded onwards. On the right side of the road was a woman walking two dogs. I had not seen her before, but she waved as I passed by. I waved back. The new mailbox I had installed just days prior greeted me on the left. Once down my driveway and parked, I remained seated in the truck for a moment to gather my thoughts.

Before heading into the house, I walked back up the driveway to check for mail. I laughed aloud at the thought of all the attorney mail I was sure to be receiving in the coming days. A junk-mail magazine, some pesky home insurance offer letters, and a yard maintenance flyer were all waiting for me in the mailbox. A dog barked as I retrieved them. The woman from up the street approached.

"Hi there."

I waved. "Hi."

"Are you new here?"

"I was going to ask you the same."

She giggled. "I'm Veronica."

Yes you are, I thought to myself. She was mid-height with black hair, olive eyes, and a near perfect complexion somewhere between tan and fair skin. The compression tights she wore brought out the nice features of her waist.

"Nice dogs," I replied.

"Thank you. You're single, aren't you?"

She was cutting to the chase it seemed.

"You must be psychic."

Her dogs sniffed my feet and legs. She tried not to laugh.

"Looks like you had fun last night."

It was then that I realized how bad I looked and smelled. After glancing downward, my shirt appeared wrinkled and disheveled, my shorts had dirty blotches on them, and my socks looked as though they came out of an old gym locker.

"Uh, kinda."

Amazingly, she was smiling. "I have time."

My mind raced to come up with one hell of a story. I grinned, realizing that I already had one.

"So, last night…"

That Shorty Sam

Glitz and glam?
Don't ask Sam
Nine to five is his work schedule
A trailer to live in and junk TV await him when he's
off

Most days were eventless for Sam
Rain or shine, things went along unhinged
Nine to five, then a trailer to live in and junk TV
awaiting
When Sam was really bored, he watched figure
skating

One day though, one day things were different
A delusional bastard broke into Sam's trailer hellbent
From watching TV, Sam stood
He warned the intruder that his decision would do
him no good

Twice Sam's height
The intruder had the visual appearance of might
He dared Sam to give it his best
If he could pass the test, beating him man to man

The intruder stood boisterous and tall
Laughter from him, Sam was after all short and slim

Face to face, Sam lunged forward
His face at crotch height of the intruder, a bite he took

Can you guess why the intruder gave a certain look?
Grabbing his crotch, the intruder fell more than a notch
Sam lunged atop the intruder, biting his neck
Privates gnawed too, the intruder's life was now a wreck

The intruder scurried off, bloody
Sam's boring life continued unhinged
Singed is the intruders dignity
Glitz and glam does not equal that shorty Sam

Old Man Digby

Ronny Harris was dating a 14 year old named Priscilla Turley. We called her "Prissy." I was 13, as was Ronny. We teased him about having a girlfriend but the neighborhood boys all secretly had a crush on her. My mom told me it was rude to call her that, so I avoided mentioning her as much as possible.

It was a Monday, and the bus was late dropping us off. Dylan Yates, Frankie Ellis, Sandra Williams, and myself got off before Ronny and Priscilla. Others on the bus "wooed" as the two exited. The skies were overcast, but that didn't seem to bother any of us until we approached a house on the right side of the street. The house was four or five down from the bus stop and was owned by a strange old guy we all knew simply as "Old Man Digby." Stories swirled around about who Old Man Digby was, and it was Ronny's older brother that claimed there were bodies buried in the old man's house. The story stuck because the house and its yard were run down and there wasn't a kid in the neighborhood who wasn't nervous when passing it.

"Hey guys," Ronny said.

"What's up?" Sandra replied.

"How long do you think Old Man Digby has lived there?"

I looked at the house. It was two stories with faded yellow siding that was badly damaged. One of the second story windows appeared cracked and the porch railings at the front entrance were in need of repair. The overgrown lawn full of thistles put the place over the top as spook central.

"Probably since before the neighborhood was here," I said.

Dylan, chewing bubble gum, shook his head. "These houses are all part of the development."

"Which makes it worse that his is so awful," Frankie added.

Prissy didn't like the gossip. "Maybe he's old and in bad shape and can't take care of the place."

"Isn't that what kids or relatives are for?" Sandra said.

"Count me out. If you mean that we should be helping him," Dylan replied.

I continued to focus on the house as we slowly passed by. There was a cat sitting inside on the sill of the window near the front door. The glare of its eyes caught my attention, spooking me. I quickly turned to face the street.

"He's been here as long as I can remember," I said.

"My brother swears that—" Ronny started.

"We know," Frankie interrupted, "I'm surprised he knows so much without knowing how long the guy has lived there."

"I'll ask my dad," I replied.

The house drifted from sight behind us as we proceeded down the street towards our houses. Ronny and Prissy departed first; they were having dinner with Ronny's family that night. Frankie's house was on the left just a few down from Ronny. Dylan's was two down from Frankie's. Sandra and I were neighbors and lived at the cul-de-sac.

"See you later," Sandra said as she approached her driveway.

My bike lay in the front lawn of my yard, and I knew that meant my parents would be upset with me. I shook my head.

"I'll be out after dinner," I replied.

After putting my bike in the garage, I headed inside. My older sister Julia was seated in the living room and greeted me in her typical rude fashion. I ran upstairs and threw my backpack on my bed before racing to the kitchen to get a snack.

"Honey, we are about to eat dinner soon!" my mom yelled from the laundry room.

I settled on sipping milk out of the carton before slamming the fridge door shut and returning to my room. Video games kept me busy until my dad came home. We always knew when he returned because of the sound of the closet door nearest the front door opening and closing. Not long after he walked in, mom called for dinner. Julia pushed me aside as we both exited our rooms to head downstairs. I pushed her from behind.

"Stop, loser!" she yelled.

"You're the loser," I replied.

"Enough! Dinner, now!" my dad barked.

I sat across from Julia at the table. Mom made lasagna, and my dad seemed a bit worn down from work. We filled our plates.

"So," dad said, "why the hell was your bike laying in the yard?"

I knew this was going to come up. "But I put it away when I got home."

"Exactly. It was out there this morning when I went to work. Explain why you deserve something that you don't take care of?"

Julia smirked and mom glared.

"I won't let it happen again," I said.

"For the millionth time," Julia replied.

Mom put her hand out. "Enough."

"How was your day, sweetheart?" dad asked.

"The clinic was busy this morning, but I made employee of the month. They let me off early today," she answered with a smile.

"Mom, that's wonderful!" Julia congratulated.

"Awesome. You deserve it!" I added.

Dad finished chewing, then smiled. "Well done. Are you really surprised though?"

Mom blushed.

"We aren't surprised. You're the best, mom!" Julia continued.

"You're all too sweet."

Dad gazed at her and the two had a moment at the table.

"So," mom continued. "As a reward, they gave me two tickets for a Caribbean cruise valid until next year!"

We congratulated her more. After a few moments of eating silently, I decided to ask about Old Man Digby.

"What about him?" dad asked.

"Ronny's brother Russ says that he killed somebody and hid the body in his house somewhere," I explained.

Mom tried not to choke, and Julia scoffed as she shook her head.

"Russ is a moron. Why do any of you twerps listen to him?" she asked.

"Darling," dad interjected.

"No. First off, Russ keeps asking me out. You couldn't pay me to date him. He's gross. I don't get why these kids look up to him," Julia added.

Dad waved his hand in her direction. "Darling."

"But dad!"

"Julia, enough. Allow me," he started. "Son, Old Man Digby is just strange. His family had a farm at the end of town back when I was growing up. His parents died and the only two known relatives were he and his sister. I think her name was Darla. They sold the place because they weren't capable of running it. Darla took her share of the money and left town. Old Man Digby ended up buying the place down the street. Leave him be. His place is rough, but that's his problem."

"I'm surprised the HOA isn't involved though. His place is filthy," mom replied.

"Yea but dad, people go to his house and don't come out," I said.

"Oh my God, do you ever quit?" Julia asked.

I stuck my tongue out.

Dad laughed. "We said the same thing about his folks when I was a kid. I still think the father was worse than Old Man Digby."

I resumed eating.

"And sweetheart, the HOA has him on a short leash. It sounds like they will be upping the ante on penalties soon if he doesn't meet compliance," dad finished.

The remainder of dinner was quiet. The lasagna was good as it usually was, but my stomach was more than just full, it was noisy! After using the bathroom, I went to my room to get my jacket and go outside. It was still light out, but the overcast sky made it particularly gloomy. Sandra's dad Gene stood out front of his house smoking.

"Hey kiddo," he greeted.

"Hi Mr. Williams."

"How's school this year?"

"It's okay I guess," I replied.

"Sandra says that you two have three classes together. Study partners?"

Gene was a tall, balding man who always wore plaid flannels and carpenter jeans. He was a nice man, so his large presence didn't come off as intimidating.

"Yep. She's smart. Glad to have help in a few classes," I admitted.

Gene puffed on his cigarette and smiled. "Do kids your age date?"

"I'm 13!"

He laughed. "Oh, yes. You're a teen, not a kid. Forgive me."

"Hi dad," Sandra said as she exited her house.

Gene turned and hugged her with his right arm. "Hey cutie."

She saw me and waved. I waved back.

"Are you two hanging out this evening?" Gene asked.

"Sort've," she replied.

Just then, Dylan and Frankie came running down the street towards us. Gene looked, then Sandra pulled his arm off her and approached them.

"What's with the running!" she yelled.

Gene laughed and shook his head. He finished his cigarette and pointed at me.

"Don't be out too late."

I nodded to him as he went inside. Dylan, Frankie, and Sandra stood in the middle of the cul-de-sac. I joined them.

"You two," Frankie huffed and puffed.

"What?" I asked.

"Like, Old Man Digby, he left. I got a flashlight so we can check out his place."

"Are you nuts?" Sandra asked.

"Russ is coming with. He has a light too. He said that Old Man Digby never locks his door," Dylan explained.

I wasn't sure what to think. In my mind I was willing to go only if we all went together. Even then, I wasn't sure it was a good idea.

"Why do we need to mess around with him?" I asked.

"If he killed somebody, he needs to be turned in!" Frankie insisted.

Sandra flailed her arms. "If we know he killed somebody, how come nobody else knows?"

"Just come with us to Russ' place," Dylan said.

I asked about Ronny.

"Ronny and Prissy, sitting in a tree…" Dylan and Frankie chanted.

Sandra laughed, then looked at me. "You two shut up. Fine, we'll come."

Sandra's decision to go meant that I would go as well, and it made it easier for me to justify my involvement. We proceeded up the street towards Russ' and Ronny's house. Russ was the same age as Julia, 15. He was tall and a bit overweight, but we saw him as brave, smart, and enviable. That Julia hated him made me admire him more as she was always a pain in the butt. The four of us chatted amongst ourselves until we reached the house, on the right. Russ' and Ronny's dad was an attorney or something like that. He wore suits to work and their house was the nicest in the neighborhood. Russ was sitting on the front porch. Once he saw us approaching, he put up his finger and ran into the house. We remained out front.

There were loud voices in the house, then Russ exited. "Okay guys, I'll be back! Ronny, you can still come if you want!"

"He's not coming?" I asked.

Ronny shook his head. "Lovebird will do anything for Prissy."

"She's a babe, but the man has lost his mojo," Dylan replied.

"She's not that great. Good looking I guess, but still," Sandra said, looking at me.

I stared back. "Guys, how do we know we can do this and not get caught?"

"Easy," Russ said, "the geezer left. He doesn't lock his door."

"What, are you neighborhood watch?" Sandra asked.

"I pay attention to detail. The guy moves slow, and I've never seen him lock the door when he leaves. When he returns he simply opens the door and enters."

"If he's a bad guy, why don't we just tell the cops or an adult that will listen?" Sandra continued.

"I'm older than all of you. I've tried. Think about how it will feel once we expose him!"

Frankie put his hand out. "I'm in, baby!"

We all 'fived, then entered the street going towards Old Man Digby's. Light remained in the sky, but it was dimming fast. Russ gave me a flashlight and kept one for himself. The group had three total. The walk towards the house was a quiet one; Russ led the way and I noticed Sandra gravitating closer to me. Dylan and Frankie mumbled to each other. After a few moments, Russ snapped his fingers and pointed to the left; there the house was. Darkened and silent. Goosebumps rose from the back of my neck.

"Guys, are we sure about this?" I asked.

Russ put his finger to his mouth, then pointed at the house.

"Hey, don't leave me here. Whatever you do," Sandra said as she clutched my arm.

Never before had she grabbed me in such a way. Something came over me. To have her on me like that felt awkwardly amazing, and it was then that I knew I wanted to go into that house and figure out what was up.

"I won't."

We gathered behind Russ and slowly approached the front yard. The bugs were chirping loudly, and the thistles in the front yard looked particularly eerie in the darkened atmosphere of late evening. I flashed my light towards the windows to see if I saw the glare of the cat's eyes.

"What are you doing?" Russ asked.

"Looking for the cat."

Dylan looked at me. "What cat?"

"I saw it when we were walking home earlier," I said.

Frankie snatched the light from me. "In the house only, fool."

"Somebody could see the lights from outside too," Sandra reasoned.

I shook my head and proceeded with everyone up the steps of the front porch. The planks creaked as we walked on them. Russ slowly reached for the doorknob and turned it slowly. The door opened!

"Told ya," Russ said, grinning.

Sandra slid herself behind me holding my side as everyone walked single file into the house. A numbness came over me as we entered and a distinct closet-type smell was present. Russ flashed his light to the left revealing the kitchen. Frankie flashed his to the right showing the living room. Dylan flashed his straight ahead revealing a stairway.

"Do we split up?" Dylan asked.

"No," Sandra said, holding me.

"Dude. The smell here is dank," Russ added.

The kitchen looked very basic, but the floors were caked with dirt and dishes were piled in the sink. There was an open cavity where a dishwasher was supposed to be, and the cabinets looked old with some missing handles. The living room had aged shag carpet with a decrepit couch and a large floor mounted TV.

"That TV, it looks like my grandparent's set," Frankie said.

Dylan laughed. "Old Man Digby is old. Big surprise,"

Sandra and I stood at the entrance between the other three. The front door remained open. Russ signaled for me to close it which I did. The kitchen was nasty, but didn't seem to reveal anything. Neither did the living room.

"Basement or upstairs, that's where the big dirty has to be," Russ said.

"We can totally leave now and be fine," Sandra insisted.

Dylan faced her. "You were willing to come this far, why turn back now?"

I pulled Sandra closer. I enjoyed holding her, and she held firm in response.

"We're good. Let's check upstairs. I'm not sure if there's a basement here," I said.

Russ shook his head. "Our houses have basements, this one must."

He led the way up the steps, followed by Dylan, Sandra and I, then Frankie. Like the porch, the steps creaked. It was now dark outside, and the decision not to have lights for each of us looked increasingly foolish. Sandra and I proceeded together depending on the other three for light. Just then, Russ reached the top of the stairs and gasped. We all screamed. Dylan turned to go down the stairs bumping into Sandra and I. We bumped Frankie who fell backwards down to the ground floor.

"Oh my God! Frankie! Are you okay?" Sandra asked, covering her mouth.

He moaned and grabbed the back of his head.

Russ flashed the light. "Sorry man, it was that damned cat."

"Told you, jerk!" I yelled.

Dylan ran down the steps. "Frankie!"

He rolled over and slowly got to his feet. "I'm fine."

Russ remained at the top of the stairs and slowly walked down the hallway. We quickly followed. In front was two doors, one on each side. Russ walked to the end of the hallway between the two. Along the right side of the staircase was a walkway to two additional doors behind us. Sandra and I went with Frankie to the first door on the right. I wanted to make sure he was ok. Russ opened the door on his left and announced that it was just a bathroom. The door Frankie opened was a bedroom. There was a queen-sized canopy bed to the left, a large mirror on wheels in the back right corner, and a large wooden dresser to the immediate right.

"That thing is caked in dust," Frankie said of the dresser.

Sandra screamed. "That bed has somebody in it!"

Russ and Dylan rushed up behind us to see. I didn't notice anything in the bed when we first glanced into the room because Frankie was waving the light too quickly. At second glance, there was a person-sized mound under the covers.

"It's not moving, whatever it is," Russ said.

Dylan pushed through the group and hovered over the bed.

"Dylan!" Sandra whispered loudly.

He poked it, then pulled back the covers. It was a person! Dylan jumped back as Sandra clutched me in distress. Frankie and Russ stood stunned.

"Wait. This is a doll or something," Dylan said.

All lights flashed on it; it was the mannequin of a woman. It had long brown hair, blue eyes, and was clothed in an eerie white bed gown.

"Why would anyone have something like this in their house?" Sandra asked.

"It's Old Man Digby," Russ answered.

"My dad told me he had a sister that nobody has seen in years," I said.

Frankie walked out. "Whatever. Nothing else in here to see."

We reentered the hallway. Frankie checked the adjacent door while Dylan and Russ checked the room across from the bathroom. Sandra and I followed Frankie again, this time the room we entered was an empty guest room full of papers. The bed, dresser, and nightstand were covered in stacks of newspapers, documents, and a few photographs. One form read "IRS" something or other, and one of the newspapers was dated May 3, 1971. Frankie found a strange photo with a man, woman, girl, and boy along with a cat. We looked at it, but it made no sense. Frankie turned it over. Written in pen on the back was "Digby Family, 1947."

"So the guy is a hoarder and stuck in the past," Frankie said.

"Why would a picture of his family mean he's stuck in the past?" Sandra asked.

I scanned the room. "Look at this room. Something is going on. Hoarding is my guess."

To our terror, we heard the front door creak open! The three of us looked at each other before bolting towards a closet to the left of the paper draped bed. We slid the door open and piled in with the random papers, clothing articles, and shoes inside. The smell was hard to bear. We slid the door shut as we held each other in horror. Footsteps sounded from downstairs accompanied by whistling. I had no doubt that it was Old Man Digby, but then I wondered what Russ and Dylan were doing. The old man began mumbling, but from downstairs it was hard to make out what was being said. Sandra leaned her face into my cheek as she sobbed with fright. I held her tightly.

"Should we try to bust out?" Frankie whispered.

Before I could respond, the cat gave off an awful screech from somewhere upstairs. Dylan hollered in pain.

"What in the!" the aged voice downstairs sounded.

I tried to cover Sandra's mouth and conceal her wailing. Frankie remained with us in the closet as we heard somebody run down the stairs.

"Who in the hell! What are you doing here, you little shit!"

"Dude, I'm out!" Dylan replied.

"Dylan!" Frankie loudly whispered.

Complete numbness overcame me. I was anything but calm, but I was beyond fear as well. I continued holding Sandra and covering her mouth. Russ seemed to remain quiet and concealed somewhere upstairs.

"You ain't goin nowhere!" the old voice proclaimed.

Dylan groaned as though he was being held, and then a scary and awkward slit noise gave way to a gasp and then thud.

"Now if there's anymore of you bastards in my house, I'm 'gon get ya!" the old voice continued.

Tears from Sandra were drenching my cheek and shoulder. I remained numb to the core. The closet was pitch black, and I could only imagine what the old man looked like, or what happened to Dylan. The old man began talking to the cat that apparently followed Dylan down the stairs moments earlier. A cabinet door opened and closed as the man continued sweet talking to the cat. Just then, a door upstairs creaked open. Footsteps sounded; they rumbled down the stairs.

"You monster!" Russ yelled.

"I knew it!" the old voice replied.

Frankie grabbed Sandra and I as we remained huddled together. Things got worse as a loud bang sounded, then another thud.

"Trespassing in my house. Never again!" the old voice ranted.

Frankie began moaning loudly. I tried to hold him in and conceal the sound. Russ groaned from downstairs.

"I'll get back to you in a minute, shithead," said the old man.

None of us knew what to do. The old man had a gun, and we could hear him creep up the stairs. It seemed only a matter of time before we would be facing death. The man began whistling in a sickly jovial fashion. He slammed open a door on the far end of the upstairs hallway and laughed. Then he slammed open another. Frankie and Sandra were bawling, and it was easily noticeable.

"Oh, so you found my sister's room? Real cute. You're over here somewhere," he said.

My head was so bogged in numbness that I couldn't muster the ability to act in any fashion. Frankie and Sandra were completely out of it and all I could do was hold them as tightly as possible. Tears began to stream from my eyes. Then, the door to our room opened.

The old man laughed. "Last but not least."

The clicking sound of a gun being cocked and footsteps over the papers in the room rose the level of terror. After a brief silence, there were two more steps closer to the closet door before the shock of a woman screaming down below. The old man gave a confused moan and seemed to proceed out of the room as someone thundered up the stairway. A pump action noise and thunderous boom gave way to yet another thud, this one upstairs. Sandra lost it and full on bawled. Frankie yelled "NO" as he fell into hysteria. Tears continued pouring out of my eyes and my nose was sweating.

"Who's up here!"

It was Ronny's voice. I bawled, then stood up and flung the closet door open. Frankie and Sandra remained. Speeding into the hallway, I saw Ronny holding a shotgun standing over the old man whose chest was blown from the gunshot. I stepped on him to reach Ronny for a hug. Snout was running out of my nose. Ronny began crying.

"Dude, don't drain that on my shoulder." he said.

Prissy ran up the stairs crying like we all were, sirens slowly began sounding in the far distance. She hugged us.

"Frankie, Sandra! It's okay! Ronny got him!" I yelled.

"Go get them Ronny," Prissy replied.

"No, I will."

I ran into the room and huddled with Frankie and Sandra again, the sirens louder and louder.

"It's over," I said.

Frankie slowly rose to his feet and trudged out of the closet. Sandra remained still in the dark. I leaned my face in and using my nose I found her lips and kissed her. She slowly got up, holding me tight once again. Adults screamed from the first floor, and Russ continued to moan on and off. Everything became a blur. I remember hearing policeman enter the house, then paramedics, and they took us outside. Russ was taken to the hospital with a gunshot wound in his side. Dylan was pronounced dead at the scene due to the blood loss of his stab wound in the chest. Using his father's 12 gauge shotgun, Ronny killed the 73 year old Delton Digby.

Sometime after the ordeal, many things came to light. Russ was correct; Old Man Digby was a murderer. He murdered his sister years earlier and excavated his parents remains to bury them in his basement, forensics were being conducted to see if he also murdered them. The mannequin in the room was of his dead sister; psychologists suspect that he made it as a way of coping with murdering her. A fourth unidentified person was also buried with the others. Russ and Ronny became local celebrities as the boys that uncovered and put down Delton Digby, the two remained very humble about things though. The loss of Dylan and the entire experience landed us all in counseling. His parents sold their house and moved away. Julia sees Russ in a different light, but this isn't a love story. Prissy and Ronny are still going steady. Frankie has taken to writing as a way to cope with the experience. Sandra has become silent, but we still hangout, and she trusts nobody more than me. I can live with that.

I remain numb about the whole thing. Sandra is on my mind often, and I think about what the future holds for us. In the meantime, I focus on sports and my studies as a way of not letting the incident get to me. I'm proud of myself, except for those nights when I'm laying in bed and out of nowhere glows the eyes of that rancid cat. Nobody ever found it.

A Child's Joy

Never discount a child's joy
Never take for granted the glow in their eyes
when happiness exists
A day dark and cloudy becomes light all
around
Pay close enough attention, and witness
resulting positive auras abound!

Positive effort fuels the joy of a child
Material fuels hallow manners and feelings
Love, true love, fuels a shimmering light from
within
A child loved has greatness bestowed upon
them to go out and win!

Small things matter most when big things get
the boast
A child picks up on more than adults realize
An aura of love, and the value of effort seen
works well
An adult applying both can do no wrong

Lack of material wealth does little to harm
inner health
A child's ability to sense truth is quite stealth
Humanity goofs this up constantly

Overcompensating for all the wrong reasons

Worse than the extremity of Mother Nature's
changing seasons
Are adults shoving objects in a child's face
Adults crying about outside issues
Adults manipulating children

Let them be
Let them see
Let them have glee
Love and effort works

Forget the toy
Foster a child's joy

At The Gate Part I

I was never a fan of any alarm that went off at 3:45 in the morning. Come to think of it, I was never a fan of any alarm, period. On a particularly chilly morning back in March 2009, the obnoxious beeping of my alarm woke me to ready myself for work. Nothing at the time indicated that the upcoming day would be any different than what I normally was to expect.

As an Aviation Mechanic Third Class in the U.S. Navy, it was odd by some measures that I was doing a stint as a gate guard on Naval Station Norfolk. A terse argument with a First Class in the maintenance shop at my home command prompted my superiors to send me off on a temporary assignment at Sewells Point Precinct. The Master at Arms ("MA's" as we knew them) and the DoD Police were always in need of help at the gates to check ID's and ensure that vehicles were up to standards to enter the base. A few months had passed since I was "voluntold" to take the temporary assignment, but it turned out to be a nice gig. There were a lot of sailors like me sent to the precinct who had rates (jobs) unrelated to Navy law enforcement.

I groaned as my alarm continued beeping. My girlfriend swatted me in the chest to get up, soon enough I mustered the energy to rise.

"Babe, turn the damned thing off," she demanded.

I cleared my throat. "Got it, got it."

The alarm was an old digital clock which was becoming more of a rarity with each passing year. As it was dark in the room, I merely swatted the top of it turning off the alarm but also skewing the time showing on its screen. Shaking my head, I proceeded to the bathroom to wash up. After a cold shower (I liked the rush cold water provided), a quick shave, and a brush of the teeth, I opened the bathroom door all the way to allow light into the bedroom. It was best to use the bathroom light so not to upset "Suzie Q," and as it was a Monday, she would certainly be in a crankier than usual mood if disturbed.

Using the scant light from the bathroom, I donned my Battle Dress Uniform, or "BDU" as everyone called them. Back then, we wore the U.S. Woodland camouflage design; a type most of us preferred. Once dressed, I laced up my polished service boots and bloused the leggings along their tops. Reaching for my service belt in the closet, I fell forward into clothes hanging on the clothing rack.

"Really?" my girlfriend asked.

"Hey, I'm trying here," I replied.

"Make sure you're home on time tonight. We have plans with Rhonda and Tim."

I shook my head. "I know. Hopefully I don't get held up on the gates."

"Whatever. Or you're snagging a drink with those guys."

"Actually no."

She rolled over onto her stomach as I approached. I kissed her on the cheek near her left ear. "See you later."

With my uniform on and buttoned up, cap atop my head, belt fastened with my baton and Oleo capsicum spray canister—"OC Spray" as we called it—I was ready. Leaving the bedroom door open a crack and turning off the bathroom light, I proceeded to the car. A couple stood outside in the cold smoking a cigarette as I repositioned my backpack on my right shoulder and nodded to them. Three parking spots down from the entryway to my apartment was my pewter 2003 Chevy Impala. A dent on the rear driver's side door prompted me to shake my head; it was a reminder of an incident the prior year in the Hampton Roads Bridge Tunnel.

The drive from my apartment in Hampton through the tunnel to the Norfolk side was an easy one at 4:15 in the morning. On occasion there would be repairs underway on the tunnel that slowed the commute a bit, but it was never enough to make me late for shift. On that morning things were smooth. Through the tunnel and three miles south was the exit for West Bay Avenue, the exit to access Gate Four onto the base. Gate Four was one of the older gates and had not yet been retrofitted with post-9/11 security hardware. It consisted of three large pillars, one on each side of the four lane road, and one large pillar in the middle that contained a guard shack. Before and after morning rush hour, there were orange barriers placed in a staggard formation to require drivers to weave to reach the guard shack. After weaving around the orange barriers, MA Second Class (MA2) Billingsley greeted me.

"Bosner. Mornin!" he said.

I showed him my military ID. "Mornin Billingsley."

"I bet you're hoping they post you up here today."

I laughed. "Yea, oh you know how much I love Gate Four."

He grinned and waved me on. "Catch you later."

Once on base, West Bay Avenue became Bellinger Boulevard. From there it was a slight right, then a left, and after a ways the precinct appeared on the right. As it was quarter to five, I was right on time. Once parked, I fastened my service belt with only the holster empty and proceeded into the precinct. MA1 Quincy, the lead petty office on day shift, nodded to me as I entered the passageway. I followed suit.

"Bosner! Hello? Did you not hear me?" a female called out.

"Oh, hi Sheardon," I greeted.

Tera Sheardon, all 5'1 and 120lbs of her, was an MA3 best known as the van driver that shuttled sentries such as myself to and from the base gates. In her hand was an OC spray canister.

"You might wanna hold on to this better next time," she said.

I stood plain-faced before she handed me the canister and patted my cheek. She proceeded towards the armory. After refastening my belt and making sure the baton and OC spray was securely placed, I approached the armory. At Sewells Point, the entrance was a passageway that opened into a room with a few tables on the left. Straight ahead were two caged windows where arms were issued; the M9 service pistol was most common. From there, a passageway on the left led to the briefing rooms.

"Bosner, what the hell man!"

I turned. It was Aviation electronics technician Third Class (AT3) Phil Scanlon, my best friend at the precinct.

"Hey, what's up," I said as we 'fived.

"You shoulda came out last night!"

We walked side by side to the second briefing room on the right.

"I'm good for once a week. The girlfriend hates when I go more than that. Hell, she thinks I do go more than that," I explained.

"Anderson hooked up with the bartender at O'Galley's."

I was surprised. "Come again?"

"Yea man. We were there at happy hour and she gave him her number."

"You're talking about Shelia, right?"

Scanlon nodded. "He went over to her place after we paid up."

We posted in formation, he and I were last and second to last in the first column.

"Lucky bastard," I said.

Scanlon grinned and nodded. A few more people entered and posted in formation before MA1 Quincy began his morning address. There was nothing particularly notable about his spiel except his remarks about one of the sentries being caught sleeping in a guard shack.

"There's no easier way to get your ass in hot water than to sleep while on duty," he began, "you all damn well know that. Unfortunately, some of our shipmates don't get the memo in time. You aren't just representing Sewells Point, or a gate. You're representing the United States Navy, and even bigger, the United States Armed Forces."

"Who was it?" Scanlon whispered to me.

I shrugged my shoulders.

"Scanlon!" Quincy called out.

We straightened up.

"I'm talking. But, since you can't help yourself, you get pier watch on Seven."

There was a collective scoff among everyone in the room. Scanlon's jaw dropped as he shook his head.

"Now," Quincy resumed, "everyone knows how we operate. Your bearing on post is half the job. No lollygagging or horseplay out there. No matter how many times we discuss this it still seems to be an issue for some of you. Standby for post assignments."

Scanlon shook his head again as MA2 Maxwell issued post assignments to us. Pier watch was considered one of the worst as far as having something to do. It was a watch that consisted of sitting in a shack looking at waves and logging what was visible every hour on the hour. The most common description in the deck log for pier watch was "all clear." I was ordered to Gate Four, which was considered the "drunk gate" on base since it was perceived as the easiest one for people to get through after a night out partying. As far as I was concerned, Gate Four was better than Pier Watch.

"Lucky asshole," Scanlon said.

I grinned. "They posted me with Ogabe."

"Have fun with that," he replied.

"Hey, I can get anyone to talk."

Scanlon shook his head as he headed to the armory to arm up for post. I followed.

"Guess what, buttheads?" Sheardon called.

Scanlon and I looked.

"I'm driving you both to your posts."

I laughed. "Lucky you."

"Who else would?" Scanlon asked.

Sheardon swatted him in the chest. "Kelly or Vincent, but they ALWAYS send you my way."

"At your request," I joked.

She glared. Scanlon neared the armory and checked out an M9 service pistol. He retrieved it from the armory tenant and loaded it from the station. Next was me. I did the same.

"Did you ever hear about the dumbass that discharged his M9 at Gate Three?" Scanlon asked.

"That was Rogers. He was sent back to his command," Sheardon answered.

I rolled my eyes. "Did they think it was unloaded?"

"The idiot thought it would be cool to twirl it around with his finger. Didn't work as he planned," she explained.

We laughed and followed her outside to the 2007 Ford E-350 Super Van. With all our gear, it was a headache to be forced to sit in the back, so we tried to hurry to the van and take up a seat towards the front. This often annoyed those who still had to push their way past us and sit cramped, often with smug faces, behind us. Making matters worse was the fact that Sheardon always dropped off the sentries sitting watch on the piers first. As the guy going to Gate 4, I was to be the last stop.

"Sheardon! Like it or not I'm the first stop!" Scanlon quipped.

He sat next to me behind the driver's seat. She looked at us through the rearview mirror.

"Watch it, I'll make you the last stop."

I laughed. "Good, let's swap Gate Four."

Sheardon shook her head. Just then, Ogabe entered the van. He was the last sentry.

"Ogabe, it's me and you today!" I said.

He glared at me, trudging his way to the last available seat in the back. Next to the last spot in the back sat MA3 Yates.

"Got ya a space right here," he said.

Yates was from Jasper, Florida and often cracked us up because of his drawl and timely wit. Ogabe simply shook his head as he took the seat.

"Ogabe," Yates continued, "looks like they got you with ol' Bosner at Four. You excited or what?"

I looked. "Yea man, you ready to have some fun?"

Ogabe looked on. "Oh, yea. Totally."

I nodded as Yates smiled and looked forward. Sheardon backed up the van and proceeded to the main street. As we approached the waterfront where all piers were located, a few of the sentries requested a stop at a store nearby. The Navy Exchange was a large base retailer, but it had smaller locations on base that served as gas stations and convenience stores, one of which was close to the piers. Rarely did any of us go to our posts without a quick pit stop.

"Fine," Sheardon said, agreeing to stop, "but ya'll need to hurry the hell up! I'm not going to take another ass chewing from Quincy about how I was late picking up the night crew."

Everybody was pleased, carrying on lighthearted conversations until we arrived at the store.

"You gonna get that sugar loaf crap again?" I asked Scanlon.

He opened the door for me. "Screw you."

"Imagine what happens when you get out of the Navy and you keep eating that shit."

Just then, someone patted my shoulder. It was Mineman Second Class Olstead.

"Yea, well you and those damn pickled sausages," she said.

Olstead was a tall, dark haired woman from Nebraska. She never specified the town.

"What, so they are shaped funny. Still tastes good," I said.

Yates chimed in. "She likes shapes like that too I bet."

Olstead glared. "Do you want to get your ass handed to you."

"From you? Maybe," he flirted.

Scanlon and I laughed, then proceeded to the aisles respective to the snacks we routinely bought. I grabbed a coffee as well. At the register was LaRonda, a short boisterous lady from old Norfolk. She regularly gave us hell at the register, but we knew it was platonic.

"Come on baby, you know those sugar loafs will rot 'yo teeth," she greeted.

Scanlon nodded. "In time sure. But maybe I'll get tired of looking this sexy and want to change."

I laughed and gestured at my figure. "Nah, this here is sexy."

LaRonda smiled. "You sweet baby. Yo woman better be treatin you nice."

"You know it," I said, though the truth suggested otherwise.

We paid for our snacks and returned to the van. Sheardon shook her head implying that we took too long. We blew kisses. Scanlon was dropped off at Pier Seven, which was void of any moored ships. Though it made the post boring, the watch was easy—so long as he did not fall asleep. Sheardon went down the line to all piers dropping off sentries, then we made our way towards the gates. As usual, the Gate 4 sentries were last. Beyond lacking the modern, 9/11-style security amenities, Gate 4 also lacked the modern security systems featured on all but one of the base gates. Once stopped, I allowed Ogabe to exit the van first.

"Aight Sheardon," I said, "you better be here on time for chow! I get hungry fast after 1100!"

"You'll get chow when I get here," she laughed.

I exited the van and walked from the shoulder on the southbound exiting lanes across to the guard shack in the median. There were two night crew sentries, Garrett and Phelps, along with a DoD cop whom I did not recognize. Garrett and Phelps gathered their belongings, signed the deck log and tipped their caps to us as Ogabe and I got settled in.

"Mornin fellas," the DoD cop greeted.

We followed suit.

"I'm Sergeant McDinney."

McDinney was about my height with a scar or birthmark on his left cheek. Boston was my first guess of his origins by the accent.

"Do either of you know when my relief will be coming?" he asked.

"DoD has their own schedule and rotation," Ogabe replied.

"Normally at 0600 or 0700," I added.

McDinney slowly shook his head. "Well, it's easy enough here. I'm surprised how few cars come through."

Ogabe laughed. "It gets busy as hell for morning rush. It's still early."

Just then, a yellow pickup approached weaving between the orange barriers placed in a staggard formation on the three lanes entering base. McDinney stepped outside to the lane closest to the shack to review. The pickup had a blue decal with month and date stickers below it on the upper center portion of its windshield. The blue decal indicated that the vehicle belonged to an officer. The gentleman driving wore a uniform with Lieutenant Commander insignia on the collars. McDinney greeted, wishing him a good day as he reviewed the driver's military ID and saluted. Two more vehicles approached, McDinney reviewed them in the same fashion. Both featured red decals which indicated that the vehicles belonged to enlisted personnel.

"I can take over first," I said to Ogabe as I put my backpack underneath the counter.

He nodded, and I replaced McDinney. Cars gradually began trickling onto base at a higher rate, then at 0530, MA1 Quincy arrived and used a forklift parked across the street to remove the orange barriers. All three lanes were desperately needed to keep traffic from backing up to the point where it slowed cars on the Interstate just a mile away. At that point, Ogabe stood on the white median lines of the second lane, and McDinney stood on the adjacent ones. I remained at front lane nearest the guard shack.

"You know there is supposed to be a third person here with you during the morning rush," Quincy said.

I faced him. "We have Sergeant McDinney."

"Don't be a smartass," he replied.

Just then, the van pulled up and out came AT2 Werland. He was an older man that joined the Navy out of passion for service to the country. We looked up to him as a father figure and marveled at his maturity, something a lot of us were still working towards. Quincy nodded in approval at his presence as he took a seat in the guard shack to serve as a rotational relief to the three of us on the street. With enough personnel, everyone was allowed a rotational 15-30 minute break. When the morning rush slowed, the extra personnel would be sent to other locations to provide relief as well as lunch breaks. The setup worked well so long as there were enough sentries detailed to the precinct; sometimes this was not the case.

"Bosner," Werland whispered as he tapped my shoulder.

I faced him.

"How's Ogabe treating you?"

"He's fine," I said, "quiet, but when is he not?"

"He hates white people. You act like you don't notice."

In a normal tone I replied, "It is what it is. Must be a reason."

"Okay, well you can take first break," Werland said.

I took a seat in the guard shack and filled out the deck log at the top of the hour, everything was clear. Rarely on the gates did anything occur that was noteworthy in the deck log. On occasion, an unruly motorist trying to enter base or someone with stars on their shoulders would pay a visit and a note would have to be added. I kicked my feet up on the counter in the shack but was quickly rebuffed by Quincy.

"I'm still here damnit," he barked.

He stood outside the window on the median facing me. I smiled and waved before putting my feet back on the floor. At that point, I snacked on some chips that I stowed in my backpack. The pickled sausage was normally my snack closer to the end of the day. Loud voices broke my zoned out state of mind a few moments after finishing the chips. I looked.

"No, no man Barry Sanders was a better running back!" Werland quipped to a motorist.

The drivers voice was hard to hear, but Werland's insistence that Emmitt Smith was the product of a good offensive line connected the dots. "You have a nice day sir!" Werland continued as the driver left.

"Bosner?" a voice called.

It was Sergeant Frankel, one of our favorites. He was McDinney's relief. I was happy to see that he would be the dayshift DoD cop.

"Frankel, how are you!" I greeted.

We fist bumped. "I heard the new guy is on post today."

"Oh, yea. McDinney. Seems cool."

"Good stuff," he replied, "I'll relieve him here in a minute. Gotta gear up!"

Frankel was a burley, high spirited man from Philadelphia. He had our respect because of his principles. Frankel never held back on supporting us when an unruly driver gave us trouble. He once chewed out a driver who accused me of refusing them entry because of their skin color. In fact, the driver had no military ID and could not confirm that their spouse was on the USS Enterprise as they claimed. Frankel made clear to the driver that they better not ever pull "the card" when nothing bad occurred. He spoke of his experiences growing up in Philadelphia and detested people "misusing the card" as he often put it.

Frankel and I proceeded to the street together. I relieved Ogabe in the middle lane as Frankel took over for McDinney. Traffic was bumper to bumper at that point. A large majority of people driving onto base had proper decals and ID and were a breeze to get through. Only three drivers during the morning caused backups in my lane. A long expired ID, missing decals, and a person that needed a day-pass to enter the base served as the culprits. Drivers requiring a day-pass had to enter through Gate 1, which was on the other side of base. Anytime a person was turned away, the sentry would take their military ID or driver's license and request the other sentries hold traffic so that the rejected driver could pull forward and make a U-turn to leave base. The ID was returned once the driver was in the outbound lanes.

"Bosner, that last car I checked, the dude was drunk!" Werland said.

I finished checking an ID and looked at him. "Huh?"

"Not the driver, but the sailor. His wife was driving him."

"Did you call him out?" I asked.

"Slipped the mind, but his command may have a word with him!"

"You know this is the drunk gate, right?"

Werland laughed. "I've heard that."

"Drunk gate?" McDinney asked as he walked towards the guard shack.

"Have a good day McDinney!" Frankel interrupted.

McDinney continued towards the shack as the rest of us laughed and continued checking IDs.

"Yea man, there's that chicken place down the street and they usually stop in there for hangover food," I continued.

"This is a pretty ghetto gate, so I can see why the boozers and cruisers pick it," Werland said.

"She's just old," Frankel added, "but she's got character."

Feeling nerdy (I always had such a streak in me), I decided to share a trival fact with the driver of a nicely maintained 1989 Camaro.

"Good morning! Did you know that the Navy has more aircraft than the Air Force?"

He showed his ID. He was a Petty Officer First Class.

"I'm a Hull Tech," he said.

"Oh," I chuckled, "you mean turd chaser?"

He snatched his ID, a somewhat inappropriate gesture, and sped off.

"Hope you have a nice day," I finished.

Ogabe shook his head. "You a weird dude."

"Bored of your break?"

"Nah, just sayin."

Werland stood between us checking drivers in the front lane. In between cars, he shook his head. "I sense a twin flame connection between you two."

Ogabe shook his head, taking off his cap and running his hand over his bald head before returning to the shack. I resumed checking IDs along with Werland and Frankel. Traffic continued to taper off as the morning rolled on, and we rotated on and off breaks. At 1100, MA2 Billingsley arrived in Quincy's place to return the orange barriers to the street in staggard formation. Not long after, Sheardon arrived with the van to drop off our relief for lunch and pick us up. Two unfamiliar MAs replaced us. One of us three was certain to be sent to another post as the gate now only required two sentries along with Frankel. Ogabe entered the van first and took the bench seat just behind Sheardon. Werland and I sat next to each other in the seat behind Ogabe. Scanlon and others were in the van as well.

"Alright snowflakes, what do you want to eat?" Sheardon asked.

Scanlon, sitting next to Ogabe, shook his head. "The snowflake is the one who drives the van all damned day!"

Sheardon gazed through the rearview mirror. "Okay, we'll take you to sewer sweet lodge to dine."

"How was that pier, Scanlon?" I asked.

"Let's not discuss," he lamented.

Yates, sitting next to Werland and I, grinned. "Seagulls be damned."

We left Gate 4. Naval Station Norfolk was the largest base in the U.S. Navy. There were numerous food courts and eateries to choose from. As we rode, a bright yellow Monte Carlo of an older year with unusually large, shiny rims passed by. Everyone looked.

"Why do people do that to cars?" Yates asked.

"Kinda stupid, don't you think," Sheardon added.

Scanlon looked perplexed. "Ah, just different. That's all."

Everyone but Ogabe had an opinion about the car; mostly negative. He appeared restless. He started jostling his cap atop his head. Just then, I made a remark that turned the day, and everyone in the van, on its head.

"Yea," I started, "must be like one of those dumbasses living in the projects on Campostella."

Ogabe glared. I continued, "They milk the system and drive their dumbass Escalades. Acting like they are special or somehow owed something."

In a flash, Ogabe's upper lip raised showing his straight, white upper teeth. Goosebumps rose on the back of my neck as he lunged at me from over his seat rest. I slid back as best I could and grabbed his arms as he attempted to strangle me.

"You cracka ass motherfucker I outta smack you in the mouth. Ignorant bitch ass!" he barked.

Scanlon's eyes bugged out. "Whoa ho ho!"

"Dude!" I yelled.

Werland pressed on Ogabe's right shoulder, attempting to get him away from me.

"What the hell is your deal?" I asked.

"You don't know them, you don't know a goddamned thing about them!" Ogabe replied.

Sheardon swerved right onto the shoulder. "All of you shut the fuck up RIGHT NOW!"

Yates laughed. "We got a live one here!"

"Bosner, what did you do?" Scanlon asked.

Ogabe swung around. "You didn't hear what his cracka ass was running his mouth about? Ya'll a bunch of ignorant fools."

"EVERYBODY!" Sheardon called, "we're armed and apparently pissed the fuck off. Imma need you all to calm the fuck down right now or I'm calling this in!"

"What's wrong with what Bosner said?" Werland asked.

Ogabe faced him. "Ya'll takin jabs at the bruhs like nobody else does anything. Talkin about them like they the bad guys. Do you know anything that they go through?"

In hindsight, my next remark threw fuel into the fire. "Dude, I have black friends."

Eyes bugged out beyond belief with a snarling look, Ogabe lunged at me again making contact with my shoulders. I reached for his neck.

"Ignorant cracka ass. You and your bitch ass remarks. Always have some snide bullshit to say about everything. I'll show you what's up motherfucka!" he roared.

"Ogabe, Ogabe! Calm down," Yates pleaded.

Sheardon called in the incident and waited for Quincy and Billingsley to arrive.

"You two are done! I'm getting you the fuck out of this van. Stand the fuck fast!" she scolded.

"Ogabe, I meant nothing against you with that remark," I said.

Facing forward he shook his head. "You have no fuckin idea."

"No, for real. What the hell was that!?" I asked.

Breathing hard, Ogabe responded, "Every one of you motherfuckers takes jabs at Campostella, or supped-up rides, or anything that is black. Not one of you assholes has ever taken a jab at any other poor fucker that looks different. Give me an example. Bitch ass fools."

"Bro I'm not racist!" I insisted.

"Shut yo ass up," he fired back.

Sheared glared through the rearview mirror. "THAT'S ENOUGH!"

There was silence. I was completely mind blown. My mind raced to try and figure out what had just happened. Everyone in the van except Ogabe seemed the same way. After what felt like an eternity, Quincy and Billingsley arrived in separate DoD police cruisers to take Ogabe and I back to the precinct. We remained silent and in front of everyone in the van. Quincy and Billingsley remained calm. Ogabe rode with Billingsley and I rode with Quincy. The ride was tense.

"Hurling racist jabs at Ogabe?" Quincy asked.

Sitting in the front passenger seat, I looked at him. "No, I was just calling out welfare queens in Compostella."

Quincy grinned. "Bosner, that's a bruh joint. They're protective of their own."

"But I didn't mean anything racist by it."

"You know how they are."

I became confused. "Honestly MA1, no I don't. Well, I thought I did, but Ogabe flipped out."

"That's what they do."

"I guess, but something in his tone. Something else is going on."

Quincy slowly shook his head. We rode silently the rest of the way. Billingsley and Ogabe arrived at the precinct before us. As Quincy and I entered, everyone glared. The black sentries had a distinctive stare, not of anger, but confusion and bewilderment. A chord of some sort was struck. I felt very comfortable in my views, but with word of the nasty argument having spread, it was clear that I stepped into a mud pit of an issue. Trying to give good eye contact and acknowledgement to everyone as we proceeded to the briefing room, I knew that I may be in some sort of hot water. I turned in my M9, and with Quincy walking beside me in an escorting fashion I proceeded to briefing room two. The door closed behind me. Standing at parade rest was Ogabe with Billingsley next to him. In front of the podium at the front stood Master at Arms Chief (MAC) Eggleston.

MAC Eggleston was a tall, slender man from Iowa. We all liked him because he had an action-hero type aura. A Bronze Star recipient, MAC served in the Gulf War. Rumors swirled that he served in the Army at that time; something he never spoke about. I stood at parade rest next to Ogabe who briefly looked my way.

"Alright boys. What the fuck is going on?" MAC asked.

"Well—" I started.

"You don't talk in parade rest, shipmate," he quipped.

I remained in place.

"It's rhetorical anyway," MAC continued, "you do realize that you are the face of this base when you're on the gates. If you cut this shit out—whatever the hell that was in the van—I'll just send your asses home for the day. Cool off and we'll forget about this whole thing. Does that work for you?"

Ogabe moved to stand at attention. "Yes Chief."

I followed suit. "Yes Chief."

"Good. Where I come from we avoid three topics: race, religion, and politics. I recommend you do the same. You'll get much farther if you do," MAC explained.

Something in me didn't agree though. I still disagreed with Ogabe's fury in the van, but something in his fury that made me curious. I wondered what would trigger such a response to a remark I made that I felt was perfectly fine. MAC let us go, and the two of us checked in any other gear we had before proceeding to the parking lot and our respective vehicles. We kept a distance. I had a lot to think about.

At The Gate Part II

After checking in my gear at the precinct, I headed to my car and drove home. It was a silent drive. The ferocity that came out of Ogabe over the verbal exchange in the duty van really bothered me. I understood that slurs and stereotypes caused anger, but what I saw in Ogabe's eyes was beyond that. Something in my gut told me that I did not know the whole story. Once back at the apartment, I tried to get over the ordeal by watching movies. Nothing seemed to help. My girlfriend added to the distress.

"What are you doing home early?"

"Got into a spat at work. They sent me and another guy packing."

"Packing? Like in trouble packing?"

I shook my head. "I'm not sure. I'll find out tomorrow."

"At least you're here early. Won't be keeping Delia and Tim waiting."

Blah, I thought to myself.

"Make sure you wear something nice. I don't want to be seen with you in something ordinary," she continued.

I nodded and then returned to channel surfing. For our dinner with her two friends I did not care much for, I wore a striped polo with some designer jeans she bought me for Christmas. We dined at some generic town center restaurant called "Billie's Roadhouse." The venue was sappy. Delia and Tim added little flavor to the experience. While the three of them conversed, I ate my overdone French dip with soggy fries and thought about how I was going to handle matters the next morning at the precinct. At some point my girlfriend hugged my side and I did my best to laugh along with everyone. What they were laughing at, I did not know.

We returned to the apartment at around 8:00 at night. I took a shower to make things easier in the morning. My girlfriend turned the volume down on the TV as I got into bed.

"Why were you so off tonight?"

I looked. "Off?"

"Me, Delia, and Tim were having a good time and you didn't seem to care."

"I was fine," I laughed, "the food wasn't."

"You always play everything off. You seem more interested in work and hanging out with those losers afterwards."

"Losers? We spend damn near twelve hours a day standing watch together. Today I got into it with someone over a misunderstanding about welfare. Or something like that."

"Who wears the uniform and arms up to stand around talking about welfare?" she asked.

"Never mind."

"I don't know why I bother with you sometimes."

I was tired and certainly not in the mood for a tense conversation. "Can we talk about this later?"

"You always want to blow things off too."

"Jesus, woman, can we do this later? For real, I have to be up at quarter to four!"

She pulled my pillow out from under my head and threw it. "You can sleep on the couch. How about that?"

For me, it was a better option than listening to her. "Okay."

The couch was good enough to get a solid five hours of sleep. When my alarm went off at its usual time, I sat upright and mentally prepared myself for the day ahead. I envisioned how everyone else may approach the situation at work; would they simply laugh it off or consider apologizing? For me, it was important to try talking with Ogabe in person to understand and rectify the schism that was created the day before. I did my best to sneakily get dresed. My attempts were dashed when a car alarm in the parking lot went off.

"Babe, what time is it?"

"Usual. Time for me to head into work."

"We're going to meet up with Delia and Tim at the mall. Don't be late."

"I'll just piss off my bosses and get off early again. Sound good?" I joked.

"You best not!"

I laughed as I bloused my trousers above my boots, buttoned up my BDU, and readied my service belt.

"This time, show our friends some decency," she added.

I headed towards the door. "Sure thing. Bye."

Delia and Tim were her friends. Tim seemed more interested in mocking me whenever I tried to connect. Delia was all about her nails, her hair, and how great Tim was. The only good thing about having them in mind was that it briefly took me away from the thought of what was to come when I got to the precinct. The drive in was quiet and smooth as usual, and the sentry on the night watch at the gate showed gratitude as they always did when they knew they were soon to be relieved. Once I parked at the precinct and exited the car, Scanlon approached.

"Bosner, my boy."

"What's up," I replied.

"How much trouble did you get in?"

I grinned. "What is everyone saying?"

"I heard they wrote you up."

"Not that I know of. MAC just had a chat with Ogabe and I."

"You sure set him off. You might want to avoid him."

I shook my head. "Actually, I want to have a word with him."

"Are you crazy? You pissed him off enough."

"Exactly. I want to know why."

We neared the precinct. Sheardon opened the door for us.

78

"Bosner. Welcome to the new precinct," she said.

"Huh?"

"Teasing you. I think you're fine. You might want to avoid Ogabe though."

"But why?"

"I told you why," Scanlon added.

"That was pretty bad yesterday," Sheardon said.

"I agree. But I don't understand. I'm going to talk to him."

Quincy and Maxwell approached. Maxwell shook his head as he tried not to laugh.

"Bosner. You're back on Gate Four. Scanlon will post with you," Quincy said.

"We haven't mustered yet," Scanlon replied.

"We don't want any trouble. We're getting Bosner and Ogabe out to post now. Too much chatter about yesterday. It's disruptive," Maxwell added.

"I mention welfare and Compostella and now everything is whack. What the hell?"

"Scanlon, are you good to post up now with Bosner?" Quincy asked.

He nodded. We both armed up. I noticed a strange contrast between the black and white MAs and sentries in the precinct. It was apparent that word of my feud with Ogabe had made it around the social circles of the precinct and that a moral verdict was rendered along color lines. I was a child during the infamous O.J. Simpson trial, but I could not help but see strange parallels between the infamous case and what I saw that morning. One faction looked at me and nodded with a grin and the other glared. Before I could comprehend the sight, Quincy signaled Scanlon and me to follow him.

"I'll be driving you to Gate Four. The night boys will be happy to get an early relief."

Scanlon and I proceeded to the parking lot with Quincy and entered a police cruiser. I sat in the back seat.

"So, Bosner," Quincy began, "most of us don't really care about yesterday, but you can't be running your mouth like that."

"I wasn't running my mouth though."

Quincy looked at me through the rearview mirror. "You know how they get with certain topics. You have to lock it up."

Scanlon looked at him. "Who's they?"

"You know what I mean."

I was unsure, if not a bit upset. "Ogabe isn't 'they' he's someone I don't know too well and I'm trying to figure out what happened."

Quincy laughed. "They're all sensitive about that stuff. You know. Don't bring it up. That way we don't have to deal with them."

Scanlon appeared confused. "Heh?"

"I want to deal with Ogabe. I want to get to the bottom of what happened," I insisted.

Quincy shook his head. "You're a strange one, you know that Bosner?"

"I guess so."

"You're a helluva sentry though. Stay that way. Keep your mouth shut."

"I agree with the sentry part," Scanlon added.

Quincy looked on. Scanlon faced forward. The remainder of the ride was silent. Once at Gate Four, we relieved the two night sentries, Willis and Paulsen. Sergeant McDinney was again the DoD cop on watch. He greeted me and introduced himself to Scanlon. I took over as the two comingled in the guard shack. Perhaps as an ominous sign for how the day was to unfold, the first vehicle to approach the gate was an old   Ford F-150 missing the front tag.

"Good morning," I greeted.

An older woman driving alone returned the salutation.

"I see you're missing a front tag," I added.

"I'm here to deliver my husband his lunch. He's on the USS Enterprise."

"The Big E!"

"Can I go now?"

She smelled terrible, and I suspected she was a junkie of some type.

"I'll need to see some identification," I explained, "also, where are your decals?"

"A decal? He served as some sort of rope thrower."

I laughed. "Yo, Scanlon, McDinney! I need you for a minute."

"Can I go now?" she asked.

"Yes, actually, I'll need your license or whatever ID you may have really quick."

She handed me an expired license. McDinney emerged from the shack and covered the lane as I turned the beleaguered, intoxicated woman around and sent her off base. She hardly seemed to notice that she was turned away. After some time on the gates, you got used to seeing anything and everything take place. I thanked McDinney as he returned to the shack.

I had little trouble permitting vehicles on base thereafter. Soon, MA2 Foster arrived to remove the orange barriers as the morning rush began. McDinney indicated that the DoD cops had new schedules and that he was on post until 1200. Scanlon and I were skeptical. We waited for the third sentry to be dropped off to help with relief coverage, but Sheardon was late arriving at the gate. Once she screeched up in the van, we waited to see who was going to be dropped off. After a few moments, we saw someone emerge. It appeared to be Ogabe. I stood on the third lane, Scanlon behind me on the second, and McDinney on the front lane nearest the shack. We looked.

"Bosner, they did not drop off Ogabe here," Scanlon said begrudgingly.

"Ogabe?" McDinney asked.

"No, he's too short. I think that's Thompson," I answered.

At closer glance, Thompson, an MA2, approached. He was armed with an M16. As show of force, the precinct would at random post people (normally MAs) with arms bigger than the M9. Presence and show of force were core principles on the Navy's "use of force" scale. If nothing else, it was a cool sight.

"Bruhs comin to bag you Bosner," Scanlon joked.

"What?" McDinney asked.

I finished granting a driver access. "Shut up Scanlon."

"Are you two okay?" McDinney interjected.

Scanlon and I looked and said "yes."

Thompson passed McDinney and Scanlon, gesturing to me. "Take your break, Bosner."

"Hi Thompson. Posting you up here with hardware are they?"

"We're short on personnel today. Take your break."

I nodded, then waited for passing vehicles to cross over to the guard shack. As I took my break I listened to McDinney. He seemed overwhelmed by base gate operations as he was always trying to strike up conversations with motorists. We were discouraged from doing so especially during the morning rush because it impeded traffic. He seemed intent on telling drivers about what his wife made him for lunch, or how big the bass was that he caught on Lake Murray (wherever the hell that was), or even worse, he told jokes that were anything but funny. I got a glance at one motorist's reaction after one of McDinney's flat jokes. The Commander appeared wholly unimpressed. McDinney waved him off and laughed, seemingly oblivious to how terrible his social skills were.

After my fifteen minute break, I asked McDinney if he wanted his. He shook his head. I proceeded to relieve Scanlon on the middle lane. Nothing notable occurred on the lane except for an 18-wheeler that I was obliged to turn away. All freight traffic was required to enter through Gate 1 on the other side of base. We closed all lanes to allow space for the truck to make the U-turn necessary to exit. The remainder of the morning was quiet, and the rush was lighter than usual. Thompson had no interest in speaking to me and it was not long before McDinney's folksy chatter to motorists became a bore. He refused breaks, so Scanlon covered for Thompson until Quincy arrived to replace the orange barriers. Sheardon arrived not long after to transfer Thompson to another post.

"It's just us three now. Looky there!" McDinney said.

Scanlon paced back and forth on the median at the guard shack shaking his head.

"I tell ya. My wife always encourages me to reach out more and be a positive influence on people around me. How do you think I'm doing?" he continued.

Standing behind him, Scanlon put his index finger to his head like it was a cocked pistol and pretended to blow his own brains out.

"You're good McDinney. Real good," I said.

"She tells me that Ned is good looking, but that she knows she can always come to me when she needs something."

"Wait, who the hell is Ned?" Scanlon asked.

McDinney granted a motorist access, then faced him. "Oh, he's an insurance agent that she attends conventions with. We get the best deals on our insurance. Hey, how's your coverage?"

"Wait, McDinney, I think that—"

I waved off Scanlon. "McDinney, it's all good. You just do you. When she goes out with this 'insurance Ned' guy, you go out and find yourself a beautiful woman. Okay?"

He seemed flustered. "Oh no no, I could never cheat on my wife."

Scanlon and I looked at each other.

"What's your wife doing on these trips with insurance boy Ned?" I asked.

"Working hard to help us save money on coverages."

Scanlon tried not to laugh. "Oh, I have no doubt she's working hard."

A slew of vehicles arrived and we helped McDinney check them; only one was turned away. We tried our best to guide McDinney to the conclusion that his spouse was not who he thought she was, but he was simply too aloof. Feeling bad, we made him take a break as we stood watch.

"What's going on with you and your woman?" Scanlon asked.

"Nothing. I'm second fiddle to her dumb friends."

"Why are you wasting your time with her?"

"We have a place together."

"Come crash at my place. Save your money."

"I'll hit you up once I get out and start college. How about that?"

"Only if you're going to Florida. That's where I'm going when I get out of this place," Scanlon explained.

"Oh, I'm a western boy. I'll probably head back that way unless I stay here. Not sure yet."

"Whatever you do, don't marry ol' girl."

I laughed. "She's more likely to marry her bozo friends Delia and Tim."

Things quieted down. Soon thereafter, Sheardon returned and dropped off reliefs for me and Scanlon. A DoD officer I was unfamiliar with arrived as we entered the duty van, presumably to relieve McDinney.

"Alright boys. How's your favorite gate today?" Sheardon asked.

"How did you know it was my favorite gate?" Scanlon replied.

I shook my head. "I'm surprised Quincy didn't pick me up."

"Ogabe is riding in the other van with White," Sheardon explained.

Yates, sitting in the back, laughed. "How ironic."

"No Kelly or Vincent?" I asked.

86

Sheardon looked at me. "Kelly is SIQ. Vincent is at the range today for his quals."

SIQ stood for "Sick in Quarters." MA2 White normally manned the front desk at the precinct. It was rare for her to drive a duty van. I couldn't help but see it as an omen that I needed to find Ogabe and talk. Everyone thought I was insane but it meant something to me to try and come to an understanding. Sheardon drove away, with only one more gate to send relief to for lunch. After leaving Gate 5, she proceeded to the food court to allow some of us to get meals. As I was not particularly hungry, I requested that she take me to the Exchange by the piers to get only a snack. A few in the van felt the same way. Scanlon got a sub from the shop inside the food court and began eating it recklessly from his seat. Yates poked fun at him. As the van left and headed towards the waterfront and the Exchange, I bounced my head slowly off the side window. People conversed as I zoned out.

As the van approached the store, Sheardon gasped. Parked on the side of the building was the other duty van. Two sentries stood in front of the entrance smoking. I was nervous and excited.

"Bosner, you're sitting your ass here in the van. I'll have someone take your cash and get you whatever you want," Sheardon said.

"Wait, what?" I asked.

"We got a pressure cooker here!" Yates joked.

"You know damn well what," she continued.

I shook my head as she pulled into a parking spot on the opposite side.

"Ogabe is with the brothers behind the other van," Scanlon said.

"And Bosner will be sitting right freakin here," Sheardon quipped.

She instructed me to give my money to Yates or Olstead and to allow one of them to buy me whatever I wanted. I handed cash to Olstead. The two left the van. Across the way just behind the other van I could see Ogabe with Thompson and some other sentries. Yates and Olstead entered the store and for a moment I felt content to remain seated. Sheardon began talking, but as quickly as I felt content, I then felt this deep urge to go out and confront Ogabe once and for all. After getting the others in the van to laugh, Sheardon looked at me through the rearview mirror and asked me if I was okay. I glanced at her, then bolted out the side door of the van to the chagrin of her and everyone else.

They muttered and mumbled as I swiftly exited and approached Ogabe and the others huddled behind the other van. I heard Sheardon and Scanlon behind me following as they mumbled. Once I passed the front passenger door on the other van, Thompson saw me.

"Oh hell no! Bosner, back the fuck up!" he shouted.

Ogabe glared, his eyes almost bulging.

"Nah man. I want to talk. For real," I said.

Scanlon and Sheardon stood behind calling my name in distress.

"Ogabe, what's up. I don't understand where all that came from yesterday," I continued.

Thompson grabbed my arm. MA3 Watkins stood at my other side.

"Bosner. You need to back the fuck off. Now," Thompson insisted.

"Dude, I get that I was smearing Campostella. I get that it was fucked up. But, that's not why you came after me," I said.

Ogabe continued to stare.

"I want to know," I continued.

"This cracka…" Watkins said.

Scanlon and Sheardon continued calling my name. Ogabe puffed on his cigarette. Thompson loosened his grip.

"I really shoulda punched you in the mouth," Ogabe said.

"Fine, but what the hell is up?" I replied.

Just then, LaRonda approached as she lit her cigarette. "What you doin with my handsome white boy here?"

"He's running his mouth," Thompson said.

"Thinks he knows everything," Ogabe added.

Watkins laughed. I felt slightly better.

"We got into it yesterday. I was ranting about welfare. Ogabe here didn't like my example," I explained.

"Bosner here comes from Happysville out in bumfuck and thinks he knows everything about everything. Ignorant motherfucka," Ogabe said.

LaRonda looked at me smiling. "Give him a break. Ignorance and hate, two different things."

"I'm not going to just apologize and hide from this. I want to know what the hell."

"You wild," LaRonda said, grabbing my side.

Ogabe and I glared at each other. A positive smirk eventually came over his face. "Come here."

Thompson let go of my arm and Watkins stepped back as Ogabe and I walked past the van to some cars parked on the outer edge of the parking lot.

"Man, I don't know you. But you weird," Ogabe said.

"I don't get any of this," I replied.

"White people usually just say dumb shit then hide in their cliques and clean up their language."

"I don't."

He smiled. "I can see that."

"Dude, I get the whole black and white thing. I don't like welfare-milkers either way. I guess using Campostella as the example wasn't the best."

"Any cracka using anything in Norfolk as an example is 'gon piss the bruhs off. Except for the military, you know this is chocolate town."

I felt weird trying to respond, so I kept things simple. "Okay."

Ogabe finished his cigarette and threw it into the grass at the foot of the parking lot as we stood between two parked cars. "White people lie through their teeth. They insist they aren't racist, but then they aren't real. They talk fancy and sweet, but then they still scrub us."

"But I don't—"

Ogabe put his hand up. "I'm talking."

I nodded.

"They hardly seem to notice," he continued, "Literally. Everyone has their own shit, but my people gotta stick together because ya'll constantly meddling with us. Handouts, fancy talk, ass kissing, then you still throw us to the wolves. You see where they put us on watch here on the base? When have they invited us out? Then you gotta ask yourself— why should any of those niggas in Compostella even bother? And don't even try to answer that. Some might get out of there, but the ones that don't have enough problems they don't need some cracka ass like you from Mars coming around and piling on."

I wanted to answer. I opened my mouth and Ogabe looked shocked to see that I was ready to verbally fire back. I did not, however. In fact, I thought about the topic. The reality was that there were people everywhere, my hometown included, who milked the system. While I never mentioned it to Ogabe that day, I never felt disdain quite the same for the people in my hometown or elsewhere that took advantage of the system quite like I did those who did it at Compostella. Ogabe may have thought that it was because I was racist, but it was more because I had a tribal mindset like most humans, and

91

in my own world it was subconsciously easier to have disdain for people doing something that everyone did when said people looked different. It never came to my mind that I was better, or they were lesser than, it was a subconscious phenomenon. All this ran through my head as I continued to give Ogabe my undivided attention.

"I don't know. You different though. I see it. We aren't friends, but maybe if you pay closer attention you might see what I'm talking about," he finished.

"Honestly. I don't know anyone from Campostella. I just see them and I don't like how they act."

"I think that's fucked up. But I get what you're saying. You're real. I respect that," he said.

"But is that where all this anger yesterday came from?"

His stare was cause for concern.

"Dude, for real," I said, "I just want to know what's up. Screw everyone else."

He nodded. "Aight."

Ogabe proceeded to tell me about his family. It turned out that his mother was American but his father and surname were from Nigeria. His mother's family was from South Carolina. His grandfather, whom he never met, was killed by a sheriff back in the early 1960's after being confused with another man. That man had raped a woman and was later caught and proven to be the actual perp. Ogabe explained how his mother's side of the family never fully recovered from the ordeal because the sheriff responsible had ties to hate groups in the area and showed no remorse for the mistaken identification and subsequent killing. Ogabe understood that there were good people of all colors and backgrounds in society, but his experience with white people was so consistently bad that he simply took no chances with them henceforth.

"That's where I come in," I joked.

He smiled. "You a trip man, for real."

"I still think you're a dick, but maybe I was wrong about you too."

He put out his hand. We 'fived.

"Respect here," he said.

"I think so too."

Sheardon called for me to hurry up as we were running behind on our watch schedule. Ogabe and I walked side by side back to the group. Scanlon and Sheardon were talking with Watkins and Thompson as LaRonda hurried back into the store. Everyone looked at us.

"You done making out?" Thompson asked.

"Yep," I replied.

"If Quincy bitches, I'm making sure he knows you held us up Bosner!" Sheardon added.

"You two gonna survive?" Scanlon asked.

Ogabe smiled. "Bosner is a weird motherfucka."

"And Ogabe is a dickhead," I fired back.

Ogabe, Thompson, Watkins and others returned to MA2 White's van. Scanlon and I followed Sheardon back to ours. Inside, Yates and Olstead teased me about the outside exchange. Olstead bought me a microwavable sandwich, but it did little good as Gate 4 was one of the only guard posts that lacked a microwave. As a joke, he got a strawberry milk, but he was unaware that strawberry milk was a childhood favorite of mine. Sheardon drove us to our posts and constantly remarked how crazy I was for forcing a conversation about the toxic argument from the day before. Everyone seemed perplexed that I succeeded in improving relations with Ogabe, and yet I never apologized. I knew full well that apologies were often overrated, especially when the issue was a matter of respect and not hurt feelings.

Back at Gate 4, Scanlon and I took turns asking silly questions to motorists as they entered. Scanlon took a liking to the question of "blonde or brunette" while I found it fun to ask drivers if they preferred "Coke or Pepsi." Occasionally a motorist might take offense to the activity of asking trivial questions on post, but they were few and far between and the hobby helped pass time. The only noteworthy driver that afternoon was the older woman who drove a yellow taxi cab whom I simply referred to was "Woman 413." I gave her that name for driving a taxi cab with the marking "413" in big black stenciling on the trunk. She would pass through a gate I was manning once a week or so, and she always remarked that she would be giving me her daughter's phone number the next time she saw me. She never did, however.

"Do you think her daughter is hot?" Scanlon asked.

"No idea. Woman 413 is pretty rough looking."

"I'm still waiting to see that fine Lieutenant again. I think her name is Salientes."

"The Puerto Rican?"

Scanlon nodded.

"She came through yesterday," I said, "you're enlisted though. Good luck with that."

"I can dream can't I?"

I laughed. "I suppose so."

"You coming to O'Galley's tonight?"

I finished checking an ID and looked at him. "Supposed to meet up with the girlfriend and her dumb friends."

"Dude, but we want to hear about you and Ogabe! The bromance."

"Ogabe is cool. Not a bad guy. We came to an understanding. That's all."

"I think it's neat."

"How so?"

"You know why I like you Bosner?"

"Why?"

"You say crazy stuff, but it's always up front. If you had an issue, I know you'd speak up. Most these people don't do that. They probably don't know how to."

I smiled. "Thanks, Scanlon."

"You still need to give us the nitty gritty!"

I shook my head. We resumed our post in silence. The day drifted on until Sheardon returned with the van to drop of our reliefs and take us back to the precinct. The ride was ordinary. Nothing was mentioned about Ogabe or myself. Watkins rode with us and talked about the ball game airing on Channel 10 that evening. Scanlon rambled about his clunker of a car needing a new set of brakes. Sheardon complained about her husband being a terrible cook. I simply shook my head and enjoyed chatter about everything other than me. At the precinct, I checked in my M9 and said my goodbye's to Quincy and Maxwell. On my way to the exit, I saw Ogabe standing with Thompson and others. We both stared.

"Hey, some of us are going to O'Galley's. Wanna come?" I asked.

They looked. Ogabe smiled.

"Nah man. Thanks though. Maybe next time."

I nodded and proceeded to the door.

"Bosner," he called.

I looked.

"Take care hoss."

"See you tomorrow, Ogabe."

Outside, Scanlon asked me if I was going to O'Galley's after all. I told him I was. My girlfriend texted me indicating that she was with Delia and Tim at the mall. I texted back letting her know some things came up and I was unable to make it. I returned to the apartment to change into civilian clothes, then proceeded to O'Galley's to enjoy a few cold ones with the boys. Anderson had in fact hooked up with one of the bartenders and we marveled at the sex they conducted with their eye contact. The boys asked me about the situation with Ogabe. I downplayed it all and just told them I was grateful to have gotten to know him and have his respect. Later that evening, I received a text from my angry girlfriend demanding that I move out, and that things were over. When the weekend came, I packed up all my things and moved into Scanlon's to take up the couch just as he offered. I had no regrets about anything that had transpired.

A Short Poem

Because, why not?

Really Is Word

Saturday night had arrived. My phone buzzed from my pocket as I was lounging on the couch. It was my old friend Reese; he was off work and wanted to hang out. There was hesitation on my end since I started on beer at around 6:00pm.

"It's good we can just go cruising or something," he insisted.

I laughed. "Cruising. What, like we're still teens?"

"Yes. I'll be there in a bit. You have no way out."

I conceded. A half an hour later, a humming followed by lights glaring into the windows of the sliding glass door caught my attention. Peering out the window of the door with a beer in hand, I saw Reece exiting his car. I raised my beer and opened the door.

"Hey buddy!" he greeted.

We bro hugged. "Reese, how the hell ya been?"

He looked about the same as the last time I saw him. 6'1 with unkept hair, a missing upper tooth, and wearing mostly black attire. After cracking open a beer, he stared.

"Yea, you haven't changed much. Been what, six years?"

I nodded. "I think so. Hank's funeral."

"The grapevine told me you came back."

"I figured."

We clanked beer cans together and proceeded to his car.

"Still driving this red clunker?" I asked.

"It still runs! Only has a hundred and eighty-five thousand on it. I'll be disappointed if it doesn't crack two hundred."

"Fair enough."

I cleared the clutter on the floors of the passenger side before sitting. Reese got in and helped put items in the back seat.

"It's good to catch back up man," he said.

"Damn right."

We began to leave when I remembered to run back into the house and grab my box of beer.

"Oh you rebel," Reese said as I returned.

"Still have twelve out of eighteen to go."

He grinned and patted me on the shoulder. "Good to have you back bud."

We left. The driveway was gravel, but due to a few days of hard rain it was particularly muddy. Reese's red rig, a 2002 Honda Civic, slumped through every puddle along the way. After a sharp left turn, the driveway eased up onto a high spot.

"You guys are going to have to regrade this driveway soon," Reese said.

"We like it to be a bog," I joked.

Once to the road, we turned right and proceeded towards town. A lifted pickup passing by going the other way nearly blinded us both with its unadjusted headlights. Reese cursed as I sipped my beer and laughed.

"So, why exactly did you come back?" he asked.

I took another sip of beer. "It was time. Eighteen years back east. The marriage failed and I wanted to change things up."

He turned up the stereo slightly. "I get it. I guess I didn't think I would see you living here again though."

"Me neither. Funny how things work huh?"

Reese grabbed another beer out of the box and threw his empty can in the back seat.

"You know you can still get busted for that," I said.

He watched me sip my beer then swatted me in the chest. "You know YOU can get busted for THAT."

"So what's good here these days?"

"Let's go check out Tommy's. Sometimes there's a cutie or two in there."

I nodded. "Cool. I haven't been there in, hell man, ten years?"

He grinned and turned up the volume. We proceeded straight on the highway until we reached the outskirts of town. There was a new housing development being built on the lefthand side where George's Auto Repair and the skating rink once was. I shook my head as Reese gestured in disappointment. The light turned red abruptly, we stopped. On the right was the old grocery store. It was still operating but the place had definitely seen better days. Homeless people stood on the corner just outside the front entrance as if they hoped to get a few bucks or snack from an outgoing customer.

"I thought the place would be doing better than this," I said.

Reese shook his head then sipped his beer. "You know how things go. Hey, the casino is booming. They built a hotel and everything down there!"

"Why aren't we going down there then?" I asked.

"We will if Tommy's is a dud."

A large banner advertising "August Days," our hometown's big annual festival, made us aware that we were now in downtown. The shops were beginning to close-up for the night and people dressed in their thick raincoats were racing to their parked cars on the shoulders. I had solace in knowing that the hardware store just to the left was still open.

"Oh, yea Marlin closed it up. Some big city company took it over. They're doing good because of the housing boom," Reese explained.

"Yippie."

After the next stoplight, Reese accelerated as the speed limit increased to 35 miles per hour. He abruptly slammed on his brakes when a golden retriever bolted in front of us followed by two teenagers.

"Damnit! Man!"

I spilled beer on my crotch. "Better this than one of them."

The teens waved apologetically as they got ahold of the dog's flailing leash and proceeded into the darkness across the street.

"We could've been busted right there. Like, for real!" Reese insisted.

"But we weren't. The night is ours, friend."

Things mellowed out on the east side of town as most businesses were already closed. All that remained open was Joy's Frozen Yogurt, a place where teens were most likely to be spotted. After another mile down main street, the obnoxious green lights of Tommy's Pub greeted our eyes. A grin came over my face as I was happy to see something that had remained the same as far back as I could remember. Reese was pleased to see a good amount of cars parked out front. He became fixated on someone getting out of a pickup parked just across the street from the Pub.

"Who is it?" I asked.

"Do you remember Hennie Upton?"

My mind drew an initial blank, but the first name started to come to my memory.

"Penny-Lunch-Hennie?"

Reese busted up. "Yes! She has two kids with Chris Banks, who left her and now has a kid with Tonya."

My eyes opened wide. We passed by the cars as Reese turned left into the back parking area.

"Wait, my Tonya?" I asked.

Reese laughed and nodded.

"Man, this loopy ass town."

"How were things back east?" he asked. "I mean, the people there are much more established. I was definitely an outsider."

"Tonya had a hard time getting over you dude. You definitely bailed."

I shook my head. "I was working a dead end job and wanted to go out and take on the world."

We parked in the far corner along a chain link fence separating the lot from a lumber yard. I chugged the rest of my beer and chucked the can into the box. Reese threw a spare jacket in the back seat atop it for concealment. He burped loudly and I patted him on the back.

"Aight bud. Let's check out ol' Tommy's."

"Let's," he replied.

I put my arm around him as we walked towards the Pub's sharp green lighting out front. Once around the corner near the front door, Tonya, with her still-petite figure, dark eyes, and brunette hair, stood with another woman as they smoked. Reese slowed as Tonya made eye contact with me. Twenty years disappeared and there she stood, with braces, a few pimples, a polo shirt that her mother used to make her wear, and the equally beautiful brunette hair and dark eyes. The memory was one I had not had in years. It stirred up some long buried feelings.

"Oh my God!" she gasped.

I nodded and grinned. We hugged.

"Look at you!" she continued. "Oh you look great!"

We stood hugging for a moment.

Reese waved at the other women whom I didn't recognize. "Hi Brittney."

A bouncer exited from the Pub and asked us if everything was okay. Tonya, still near-ecstatic to see me, nodded and pulled me into the Pub. Brittney and Reese followed behind. Inside, the place was the same as I remembered it. To the right was a shuffleboard table, in the middle of the open area was two billiard tables, then on the back wall and along the right side wall were tables and seats. The bar was to the left, and with it was a modest crowd. Tonya hugged me again.

"I can't believe you are back! You didn't say anything either!"

"It was a spontaneous decision," I said.

Reese patted my shoulder. "This guy hardly told me. I had to come pick his ass up from his folks' place."

Brittney, whom I didn't recognize, stood to the left. "Yea, and he obviously forgot me."

I looked at her. "I'm sorry?"

"Dude, Brittney Coreland," Reese butted in.

After a second, I recalled.

"Brittney, you look really good. I've been gone for years," I laughed.

"She got the weight loss surgery," Tonya explained.

Brittney smiled and nodded.

"Good for you. You look good. Sorry for the lapse in memory."

"Hey," Reese started. "She still talks to me!"

He put his arm around her. She took it off. Tonya and I laughed. The four of us sat near the corner. Reese continued to try with Brittney who didn't seem interested in the least. The girls ordered fancy cocktails while Reese ordered a beer and I ordered a boilermaker.

"I heard you got married," Tonya said.

I nodded. "I was. Didn't work out though."

"You know you're still good looking, right?" Brittney asked.

Tonya smirked at her and put her hand in my lap. "Yes, I was sad when you left. A lot happened."

Reese sipped his beer and laughed. "Yea, kids happened."

Brittney slugged him in the side as he continued to laugh.

"So yea, I had two, then I made the mistake of getting involved with Chris Banks. Had another."

"Your kids are adorable," Brittney said.

I had no doubt they were. Tonya was still a catch. Looking at her stirred up a lot of memories. Reese continued his best efforts with Brittney while Tonya gave me her undivided attention. We talked about the past 18 years, and how the parents were doing, and what I was doing in town going forward. My responses were short, and I tried my best to steer the conversation in a different direction. The truth was that I didn't know what I was going to do. One of the main reasons I returned to town was because of the current social climate of the world; the pandemic in particular.

"I was all about the big time stuff. Extensive travel, fancy job, fast motorcycles, fast women, anything exotic," I explained.

Tonya gazed into my eyes and slowly nodded. She was distracting me more and more.

"And after the marriage fell apart, and the pandemic happened, I never had to go into work. Everything was online," I continued.

Tonya leaned toward me. I followed suit. The kiss was everything I hadn't had in the longest time. Reese and Brittney's voices were muddled, and the loud music in the bar became dull and irrelevant. I pushed Tonya back toward the wall while our lips remained together. She moaned.

"Yea, uh, we can definitely do more of this in a little bit," I said as I pulled back.

Her eyes were big and full of passion. She seemed mesmerized. I wasn't too far behind.

"To hell with this," Reese said as he leaned in towards Brittney.

"Damnit," she replied. "Fine."

Reese and Brittney kissed and flirted around while Tonya and I sparred with eye contact before resuming our conversation.

"You remember Chris don't you?" Tonya asked.

In fact, I did. He was a friend back in middle school, but in high school he drifted into cliques while I remained independent and kept mostly to myself. I nodded.

"He played that 'sweet man' game until Dominic was born. After that he totally went off and started messing around," she continued.

"That has to be tough."

"You never had kids or anything? Why not?"

I scoffed and took a sip of whiskey. "I was focused on getting the career up and running. Then once I did that and got with my now-ex-wife, I wanted to do that stuff but her and those city folks were all about the night life."

Tonya grabbed my thighs. "You know here these girls…"

"Yep. I know," I laughed.

"Okay you two," Brittney said.

Tonya and I looked. Reese raised his glass. "What if we take this down to the casino?"

"You're gonna take that and finish it right here!" a voiced shouted.

It was Nick Rowland, an old friend of Reese's and mine. He was tall just as I remembered him with large ear gauges and a nose piercing to go with his thick frame and buzz cut. We hugged.

"Dude, when did you get back to town?" he asked.

I patted him on the back. "A few weeks ago. Haven't been out much."

"Now he's out getting back with Tonya!" Brittney chided.

Reese raised his glass again. I laughed. "We're catching up."

Nick playfully fist bumped me in the chest then greeted Tonya.

"Watch out for this guy. No telling what baggage he has."

She laughed. "I know. I have a blind spot when it comes to men. But this one, he was the original."

"So what's going on tonight?"

Everyone looked at each other.

"Really?" Brittney asked.

"We could go down to the casino," Reese suggested.

"Hell no. I was just there. Dead as hell tonight," Nick replied.

Tonya looked at me. "We could go to my place. I have Dominic tomorrow but the other two are with their grandparents for the week."

Everyone perked up at the idea. Reese got up and put his hand on my shoulder.

"See? Everything clicks when you're in town. Welcome back!"

I smiled. "I guess."

Nick approved of the idea as well and gathered his female companion from the shuffleboard table where she was winning against another woman. He had a sleek orange 2018 Dodge Ram 1500 Hemi 5.7 litter and invited Tonya and I to ride with him. We both decided to do so as Reese shook his head. Brittney left her car and rode with him.

"Alright everyone," Nick said. "This is Gemma. Gemma, this is everyone."

Tonya laughed. "I know Gemma, Nick."

Gemma was familiar, and after a second I remembered her from Biology class senior year. The only thing different about her was her short hair.

"Wow. I haven't seen you in years," she said.

"You went off and fought in Iraq huh?" Nick added.

"Oh no. I was in the South Pacific."

"You know Mr. Eller's son fought in Afghanistan, right?" Tonya asked.

"Yea he actually joined up right after I did. I went blue, he went green," I said.

Nick looked at me through the rearview mirror. "Crazy how everyone did their own thing. And yet here we are!"

Tonya sat up against me with her legs stretched on the seat space to our right. "Yes. Here we are."

The drive to Tonya's was quick. She lived east of town just off the highway on a shared driveway with three other houses. Her parents let her stay there as they had bought a place down south to avoid the constant rainfall. Memories kicked up of us at the house as young teens when we had to sneak kisses, and holding hands was a big deal. Her parents were good people, and I couldn't imagine them being any different than they were when I last saw them, albeit for their age. Nick sped down the highway to show off the power of his Ram pickup while Gemma held fast to her seat. Tonya put her arm around my waist.

"Really good to see you," she said.

I leaned into her and rested my head against hers. "You too."

A few miles later we turned right onto the shared driveway, a nicely graveled stretch of road with a small bridge crossing a large creek. On the right side was an independent driveway with a mailbox, address plate, and large wood carved sign that read "Penderson," Tonya's last name. She instructed Nick to park anywhere on the gravel, to which he parked up against the garage just to the side of the house. Reese's headlights glared into Nick's rearview mirror as he and Brittney arrived. Tonya nearly fell face first into the gravel when her footing slipped on the step bar.

"Whoa there Bessy!" Reese called out as he exited his Civic.

She gasped. "Jesus, that was close."

"Shoulda held on to me," I teased.

"You know, I'm not sure if I've been here before," Nick said.

"Oh yes you have. Senior year I threw a party when my parents were out of town. You definitely stayed the night here," Tonya explained. She unlocked the front door shoving it open. "I swear, this door."

"This is a big house," Gemma said.

Once the foyer light was on, I walked left to turn on the living room light in the corner. When the kitchen light was also turned on, the house was well lit, spacious, and almost just the way I remembered it. I smiled.

"I'm not sure what my folks will say when I tell them that you stopped by," Tonya said.

I looked at her. "I hope they're doing well."

"Of course they are. Pops is mastering his golf swing and mom is—mom is mom."

"Aight, where's the booze?" Reese asked.

Tonya went into the garage and returned with a large bottle of bourbon. Reese smiled and rubbed his hands together.

"And yes, everyone can stay here tonight," she said.

We sat on the couches and conversed. Tonya talked about her kids, and how Dominic was the hardest to raise because of Chris's antics. Gemma mentioned that she had a miscarriage some years earlier and never had the heart to try for kids again. Brittney implied that due to her prior obesity she was a virgin, but since her surgery she was having fun playing the field. Nick did a stint in the Coast Guard, which I found odd since he was once quite overweight.

"Who says I couldn't have lost weight, served a term, then got out and gained some back?" he insisted.

"Hey, hey, I'm not saying you didn't," I assured him.

Everyone took shots. Reese resumed his prowl of Brittney who now seemed interested. He also told us about how he was trying to get hired at the Correctional Facility in the next county over. The pay was well above average for jobs in the area. Oddly enough, Reese, Brittney, and Nick went into the back bedroom to "play." Gemma was aware that Nick was bisexual, but she herself wasn't. Her along with Tonya and I remained on the couches while the other three made noise from the bedroom.

"Yea, they better clean up. That's all I'm gonna say," Tonya said.

Gemma shook her head. "Brittney is a freak."

"And the other two aren't?" I asked.

Gemma smiled and poured herself another shot. "You're quite the straight shooter aren't you?"

"I'm definitely a plain kind of man."

Tonya threw a pillow at me. "Well I liked it."

"I liked it too."

Gemma laughed. Tonya pounced on me.

"Okay okay I'm not watching this," Gemma said as she faced away.

"But you left. Now you're back, but you seem lost."

Gazing into her eyes I nodded. "Things are off these days for sure."

The door to the back bedroom swung open and a naked Nick came running out yelling. A naked Reese and Brittney followed.

113

"Damnit!" Tonya yelled. "We're going to my room!"

Gemma, Tonya and I ran to her room and shut the door.

"Lock it!" she demanded. I did so.

We had the bourbon in our possession. The three of us lay on Tonya's bed passing the bottle around. Tonya clutched me on the right and Gemma clutched me on the left. The other three remained rowdy in the living room for a time before Reese knocked on Tonya's door asking about the bourbon.

"No! If you want to be freaks in my house, you can sober up!" Tonya demanded.

Reese whined at first, but eventually gave up and the three returned to the back bedroom.

"I'm so glad you're here tonight," Tonya said as she held me tighter.

I kissed her on the head. "It's good to see you Tonya."

"Don't leave again."

Her eyes closed and her breathing became deep and slow. Gemma was lightly snoring. I took a sip or two more from the bourbon before laying it behind Tonya and nodding off. Rain fell that night but by morning it was merely overcast skies outside. Gemma woke early and went into the living room to watch TV. Nick joined her. Tonya and I stayed in bed and reacquainted ourselves sexually. She nibbled on my ears which brought me back to a time long since passed. She was the only woman I had that did such. Love with her was something I missed over the years and at that moment on that morning in her bed it became clear that she was someone I missed while I was gone. I did my duty with her on that morning, and she couldn't have looked more pleased.

Eventually I rose from the bed and went to get a glass of water. By then, Reese joined Nick and Gemma on the couches. Tonya and I were loud but the three of them seemed to understand that what her and I did was beyond critiquing. When I returned to the bed Tonya had put sweatpants on but remained topless. I had nothing but my boxers on. We held each other for a bit longer.

"I got to have you again," she said.

"Yes."

Just then, a phone buzzed from the floor on Tonya's side of the bed. She slouched over and grabbed it. Her moan made clear who it was.

"What's the problem?" I asked.

"Chris is almost here with Dominic. We have to clean up."

"Is he early?"

She nodded. "Always does this. He loves to be difficult."

We both quickly made the bed and let the other three know that we needed to leave as soon as possible. Everyone quickly gathered their things. Tonya's phone buzzed again, then the sound of a vehicle barreling up the driveway meant we were too late. She ran outside while the four of us stood facing each other. Raised voices outside accompanied by a young child crying prompted us to go outside. On the passenger side of a gold SUV stood Chris, yelling and gesturing aggressively at Tonya, little Dominic dressed in a thick coat with sweatpants and rubber boots crying, and Tonya screaming back at Chris. He turned his attention to us.

"What are these assholes doing here? Wait, you're back?" he asked.

"Hey, there's no need to do this," I replied.

"Tonya, you think you can just throw orgies at the house when our son is around? What is wrong with you, you bitch!"

Gemma and Brittney intervened. Tonya was in tears yelling back at Chris. Nick, Reese, and I stood unsure what to do. Suddenly, Chris lunged at Tonya. Gemma tried holding him as Reese, Nick, and myself jumped in to stop the confusing melee. After hearing Dominic's crying initially, it became drowned by adults yelling and crying and grunting. Gemma pulled Tonya back as Nick and I held Chris while demanding that they stop immediately. Everyone was so focused on Chris and Tonya that our hearts sank when Reese and Brittney called out for Dominic. Tonya and Chris ceased arguing and began calling their son's name. Nick went around the house. Gemma looked around the cars. Reese bolted down the driveway and then right towards another house. Brittney followed and checked the yard of an adjacent lot. By sheer luck, I saw a flapping jacket hood and black hair bobbing up and down behind the foliage separating the lawn from the main driveway. Dominic was running towards the highway. I was in my mid-thirties. On that day everything I had ever done flashed before my eyes. I saw a little child, hair blonde as can be, running through fields looking at eagles swirl in the blue sky. Then came the teen on his bike racing his friends on trails up in the National Forest. Junior varsity football games, mostly sitting on the bench. A first kiss. High school graduation. Military service. College. Marriage. Esteemed career. Divorce. Isolation. Alcoholism. Then, a return to where everything started, also Tonya. When I opened my eyes, I heard faint yelling behind me. In front of me was the shoulder of the highway, and on the yellow median lines stood little Dominic.

A car locked its brakes and skid by barely missing the little boy. Everyone sprinted towards the highway screaming for mercy. To my right sounded a deep, terrifying horn. A truck with its trailer filled to the brim with logs approached fast. I bolted forward pushing the kid, then shoveling him with my hands slightly into the air so that he would be on the shoulder. A majestic flash occurred, then a thunderous boom in conjunction with organic material being smushed by a steel mass trying to halt immediately from traveling at 60 miles per hour. Time seemed to stop, but then a child cried. Through my fading vision I watched a familiar woman cry profusely as she ran to the child's aid. A man crying just as much followed suit. Two men and a woman stood over me covering their faces and sobbing. A person emerged from the truck cab and one from the halted car as well. My vision continued fading until it reached a permanent and silent darkness.

The Lead Up

The Sun rises and the Sun sets
Everyone out there could care less
The door was shut, we were all alone
Scared like hell, and chilled to the bone

Why is it we are scared
It is a stupid dream
It can be repaired
We can be redeemed

We opened our eyes and we were not
We heard a bomb that had been dropped
Screams go out, shuffling go the feet
Fate does what it wants, never missing a beat

This is so dumb, what did we do?
We wanted peace, and we loved you
If you want war, then so be it
When we bomb you, you'll throw a fit

May the best one win and the other eat shit

Blue Ridge Riders Part I

Waltz roared up beside me and patted the fuel tank on his brand new 2011 Harley Davidson Road King. We were cruising west on Interstate 66 passing into Warren County, Virginia enroute to Front Royal. I was fine with stopping to get fuel since I had a "peanut" tank on my 2007 Sportster 1200. A good rule of thumb with peanut tanks was to fuel up as often as gas stations appear roadside. Nodding to acknowledge Waltz, we took the next exit at a place called Linden on the northern reaches of the Blue Ridge Mountains.

Leaves sporadically fluttered in the air, indicating that September was almost over and the foliage would soon be orange. The sun glared and the air was crisp; perfect for riding. Once off the Interstate, we turned left onto an access road and stopped to fuel up. A woman in a minivan stared as we approached the gas pump. Our leather cuts featured our club name and colors; Bones and Wheels MC. The logo consisted of grey crossbones inside of a motorcycle wheel with an orange outline. Beneath the logo was a "Virginia" bottom rocker displayed in orange font. Waltz revved his bike one last time before cutting it off at the pump drawing the attention of everyone standing out front.

"Yo," he said.

I nodded at him. "Whassup?"

"We're gonna be late."

"Not by much. I doubt that the other fellas will be there when we pull up."

"Prez wanted to talk to me before the meet," Waltz explained.

"Don't worry bud, we will be there with time."

We entered the store to pay for gas. Customers stared. Waltz was 6'2, 230lbs wearing a black bandana over his bald head, a knife in his jean pocket, and wallet chain in the other. The women normally paid him more attention than me, the 5'9 "kid" with a full head of hair weighing a slim 165lbs. The female cashier fixated on her newly done nails until we approached. After giving Waltz a good look, her eyes locked on me. Waltz gave her $15 and headed out.

"Hi hun. Filling up too?" she asked.

She was a blondie with sky blue eyes and juicy lips.

"You know it. $10 for me."

"Are you old enough to be in an MC?" she joked.

"They haven't carded me yet."

She laughed. My eyes roamed past her necklace to her breasts then to her name tag. She looked at my name patch.

"Ok, Doozy."

"Catch you later, Renee," I replied.

We exchanged eye contact until Waltz waved at me to hurry up. Renee continued staring as I proceeded outside. Waltz finished up as I began pumping gas.

"Are you gonna come back for her or what?" he asked.

I put the nozzle into the tank. "I might. There was some heat there."

The pump clicked off at $8.74, Renee stared through the window. I blew a kiss. She waved as Waltz roared off, I followed suit.

"Keep the change, baby!"

Linden was about eight miles from our destination. We stayed on the side road as it meandered parallel to the Interstate. There was a bite to the air on the shady portions of the road as it weaved under the overhanging trees. Waltz rode in front nearest the yellow line. The purr of the bike on the open road and the air gusting past my ears had a drug-like effect on me. My vision of the road and its turns never left consciousness but worries always did. As we rounded a long turn around a timbered knob, a deer stood hesitant in the roadway. Waltz veered left while I veered right. The deer remained still, staring as we continued.

We topped a steep hill that gave way to the first stop light of Front Royal. At the green, we proceeded. Passing us going the other direction was a formation of riders. Waltz and I reached out with our left hands to acknowledge them; they followed suit. Once into downtown, we turned left onto U.S.

340 and rode south. My tinted ride glasses barely kept the sunlight at bay as we now rode into it. The final light in town was red, so I pulled up beside Waltz.

"Doozy!" Waltz called over the rumbling bikes.

I nodded.

"You got your dues, right? Ain't no ATMs this way!"

I nodded again. "Yup!"

The light turned green, and off we were. Two miles south on U.S. 340 led us to a gravel driveway on the left. After turning, we rode three quarters of a mile up the slopes of the Blue Ridge to a large property. We parked in front of a sizable brick home featuring a large shop-style garage to the right. It was the house of Hacksaw, President of Bones and Wheels MC, Blue Ridge Chapter. Waltz and I were the seventh and eighth riders to arrive. There were 17 total in our chapter.

Waltz cut off his bike as I played with the gears on mine. It was sometimes difficult to shift into neutral as the clutch would skip and go from first to second gear. Hacksaw's wife Tara stood on the front porch waving at the two of us. I waved back, then successfully got the transmission into neutral before cutting the Sportster off.

"Doozy, Waltz!"

It was Hacksaw's son Christopher. He was eight, and we made it a point to watch over him as uncles and to show him only the best.

"Christopher, you silly bear. Come here!" Waltz greeted.

He ran around the house as Waltz chased him, growling.

"Hi Doozy. How was the ride?" Tara asked.

"Howdy dear. Great ride, the weather this time of year is the best!"

She smiled. "There's coffee inside."

I removed my helmet and placed it over the plate on the rear of the Sportster before heading in. Tara held the door open. She made no secret about liking Waltz and I the most out of all the brothers in the MC. In the living room, her daughter Lena sat in a reclining chair solving a crossword puzzle. She was 12, and the spelling bee champion of her middle school. Staying with them was an older cousin whom I never met before. She looked to be in her late-teens and was going to babysit the younger two. We waved at each other as I followed Tara to the kitchen. She poured me a cup of coffee as I greeted the other brothers standing nearby.

Belcher, the Treasurer, hugged me first. I gave him $25 for my monthly dues before greeting the others. Crud, the Secretary. Zany, the Vice President. Razzle, Vin, and Tank—the biggest man in our Chapter—members. After sipping on coffee and small talking with the them, more bikes roared up the driveway and into the parking area out front. Hacksaw entered.

"Alright boys, to the shop!" he said.

Waltz entered carrying Christopher and plopped him on the floor near the recliner where Lena sat. We left the house and quickly greeted the brothers who just arrived as we went into the shop. Hacksaw had two additional bikes, one of which he was in the process of rebuilding. In the corner was a ring of fold out chairs and hanging on the wall behind was a large, black "Bones and Wheels MC, Blue Ridge Chapter" banner. Hacksaw called the meeting to begin. Waltz, the Sergeant at Arms, made sure that the shop door was closed. The 11 members present took their seats.

There was nothing noteworthy about the meeting except Hacksaw's announcement that Snazzy, the last living Founder of the Blue Ridge Chapter, passed away. The news came as a bit of a shock. Snazzy was more than just a Founder of our chapter, he was a Purple Heart recipient from his service in the Vietnam War.

"We'll be holding a gathering in his honor tonight, as some of you know. Plan to stay on the Rappahannock side. We're gonna ride Skyline Drive to Thornton Gap, then down to Sperryville. We'll meet Silver Slayers MC at Guildy's Tavern, then ride to their clubhouse," Hacksaw explained.

Everyone remained silent with a somber posture. The news was heavy; a ride was more than appropriate. The meeting ended quickly after Hacksaw broke the news as nobody had any new business to bring up. Most of the brothers, myself included, were veterans and it had special meaning to see one of our own off in a signature fashion beyond just the MC customs. We slowly exited the shop. The brothers with old ladies told them to get ready for the ride.

"Waltz," Hacksaw called.

"What up Prez?" he replied.

"Is your pal working the gate at Skyline today?"

"Cal should be up there. Easy passage."

Cal Tucker was a drinking buddy of Waltz and I outside of the MC. He was a park ranger at the toll booth on the Front Royal side of Skyline Drive. Some of us had passes as veterans. For an uninterrupted ride, we depended on connections like Cal to allow us privilege where we weren't willing to simply "take" it. The brothers fired up their bikes as Lena, Christopher and their babysitting cousin watched us through a window from inside. Tara emerged with her leathers on and as such she was Hacksaw's old lady, "Loveflame." Everyone was mounted with bikes rumbling when the Road Captain, Ironside, proceeded forward signaling everyone into staggard formation. We were off!

Down the driveway and right onto U.S. 340, we rode toward Front Royal a short ways before taking another right onto Skyline Drive. Riding near the front of the pack, Waltz bobbed his head. Cal was at the park entrance; we were going to be able to ride through unhinged. The park entrance gate drew closer as I rode in the middle of the group. Cal stood outside his booth with his park service hat and

126

pressed uniform, mustache dark and trimmed. He waved and I followed suit. The centipede that was the 11 brothers of Bones and Wheels Blue Ridge Chapter roared upward on the famously winding road atop the peaks of the continuous Blue Ridge Mountains.

The particularly nice day beckoned riders atop the Blue Ridge, and after the first major hairpin turn that the brothers all leaned through well, we approached the Shenandoah Valley Overlook on the right. Visitors and their children stared at the roaring spectacle as we passed. Lines of cars were parked up the road which soon revealed a crowd of people snapping pictures at black bears rooting in the leaves on the sloped right hand side. A few bystanders appeared annoyed by our presence passing by. Zany, near the front of the pack, made a peculiar hand gesture towards the people as they stared. I grinned.

We proceeded on the winding road past the common turnouts Fox Hollow Trail, Hogwallow Flats Overlook, and Elkwallow Gap—which featured a visitor center and snack shop called Elkwallow Wayside. Two brothers turned into the parking area but waved us on to continue. We did. As it was midday on a weekend, there was a good number of people out and about. Ironside greeted riders traveling the opposite direction. My cheeks began to tingle from a breeze that picked up as we meandered away from timbered areas. After a ways, Ironside and Hacksaw guided everyone into the turnout at Jeremys Run. By my estimation, we were near Thornton Gap. Everyone came to a stop at the turnout and cut off their rides.

"Alright, we'll chill for a minute. Gotta wait for Vin and Razzle," Hacksaw announced.

Crud, to my left, shook his head. "We hardly left, and they needed to make a pit stop."

"Vin is hungover," Waltz said, "And Razzle's butt probably hurts."

Hacksaw glared, "Huh?"

"Educated guess."

"Waltz knows all," I joked.

"I figured you and Waltz would be hungover. You guys roll with Cal a lot don't you?" Crud asked.

"Not lately. Plus he doesn't ride," I answered.

Waltz nodded. "He's good for driving cage."

Hacksaw laughed. "He would be more useful if he had a truck and not some sporty piece of shit."

Zany approached. "We can't stay too long. The 'Slayers are waiting in Sperryville. I spoke with Quicky.

"Already?" Waltz asked.

"It's all good. We will be there in thirty. As soon as Vin and Razzle get here," Hacksaw said.

"How many of the Slayers are we meeting up with?" I asked.

"Quicky said there were seven of them coming," Zany replied.

Waltz put his hand over his brow. "I think I hear the brothers coming now."

Gradually, two bikes rumbling in the distance sounded from the direction we came from. We mounted our rides as Hacksaw kissed Loveflame. They mounted as we started up. Ironside signaled everyone to proceed to the road just as Vin and Razzle, on their blue and green rides, appeared from around the corner. In smooth transition, the 11-ride centipede resumed. After a few mild turns left and right along the ridge, we approached the Thornton Gap exit onto U.S. 211. The park ranger exited his booth wearing his bright hat to gaze at the exiting spectacle. I gave the ranger a mild salute in passing to which he nodded back.

U.S. 211 was particularly dangerous because of the numerous hairpin turns going over the range. As we were at the summit already, we were descending eastbound towards Sperryville. Ironside carefully tracked the yellow line while maintaining enough space so that any passing motorists were unable to clip anyone with their protruding mirrors. Luckily, I was on the outside nearest the guard rail. Turns one and two went smoothy but Waltz braked abruptly on the third turn and Tank swerved into the oncoming lane to avoid striking him. My heart stopped. There were at least four more serious turns to go.

Tank, being the big man that he was, needed the most space to slow down. After swerving into the oncoming lane, he quickly braked and then got back into the staggard formation just before an oncoming SUV approached. Waltz looked back at Tank and apologetically gestured. Tank shook his head. A strong gust caught my face just right as we rounded a knob. My eyes teared up and I desperately tried to rub them out. In a split second, my compromised focus led me dangerously close to Crud on my left.

"Doozy! What the hell!" he shouted.

I quickly regained composure. "Sorry man!"

Crud focused onward rolling his lips while I blinked my eyes in the hopes of lessening the blur from the forming tears. I quickly remembered a story some of the brothers shared about a rider they knew who died going down U.S. 211 to Sperryville. Someone was showing off their new sports car to a pretty woman and was drifting through turns. They clipped the rider who was thrown from his ride and passed away while being transported to the hospital. The incident occurred at one of the last turns going down the ridge. I wondered which turn it was but then the rumbling of our collective rides began to put me into a riders hypnosis. Quite suddenly, everyone in front braked aggressively as Ironside swerved around an object in the lane. The streaks of purple and red on the pavement indicated it was roadkill. A dead raccoon; hazard enough to be weary of.

After a long modest turn to the right, there was a long stretch of small veering turns in both directions. I thought back to the story of the rider and quickly became aware of which turn it had to be—upcoming was a hard right. Ironside, and then Hacksaw just behind him on the right, veered quite far into the other lane. My heart pounded because of the inability to see around the embankment. Paranoid, I stayed parallel to the guard rail and remained tight on the turn. Everyone else followed more precisely with the group. At the turn I let off the throttle, braked, leaned right, then accelerated. The navigation was successful.

A few members glanced around as we passed through the turn which fueled my speculation that the accident occurred there. The road straightened out and on the right was an old brick home with smoke billowing out of the chimney. The tough stuff was behind us. After another mile or two, the road meandered into Sperryville. A quaint, very southern style community, Sperryville was excellent in the autumn as far as foliage and rideability. Shops rarely stayed open for long, but Guildy's Tavern was a mainstay and a biker favorite. Sure enough, as we approached the rustic old building, seven bikes sat parked side by side. Ironside signaled us to turn in.

There was limited space in the gravel parking lot for all the bikes. Ironside led us between the parked bikes and the deck lining the front of the tavern where we parked on the side facing the small but rapid Thornton River. Onlookers stared as the rumbling gradually ceased with us cutting off our ignitions. My leg cramped as I put out my kick stand and stood.

"Damnit," I said.

"You gotta do stretches hoss," Crud joked.

I smirked. "Maybe."

Waltz smacked my back. "Dude, you took that turn really tight up on the ridge."

"I didn't like how everyone veered on the centerline and into the oncoming lane." I replied.

"Ironside goofed a little there, that's the turn where Yuppz got smeared," Crud said.

I felt proud that I was able to guess the turn that the infamous accident occurred.

"Who was he?" I asked.

"Sergeant at Arms for the Valley Bandits," Ironside interjected, "Sorry about that wide turn up there. I misjudged a little."

We nodded.

"Bones and Wheels!" a voice shouted.

Leaving the tavern and trotting across the deck to the parking lot was a tall, burley man with long white hair and a handlebar mustache. It was clear from his cut that he was part of Silver Slayers.

"Mutt!" Hacksaw greeted as the two hugged.

Crud, Ironside, and Zany approached the two and exchanged hugs with Mutt as well.

"Do you know Silver Slayers?" I asked Waltz.

He nodded. "Yep, we're tight with them. Good guys. They knew Snazzy well."

Mutt proceeded towards the tavern, then Hacksaw and Loveflame followed. Hacksaw waved at us to come. Guildy's Tavern was neat, it had plank floors and a basic design with tables in the front and the bar in the back. Whenever I was there I felt like I was walking into a Civil War scene where blue and grey soldiers were throwing down drinks after a hard

132

day's battle. With the eight Silver Slayers members (including three old lady's) and our 11-man crew, the few regular customers in the venue quickly finished their drinks and meals and paid up. In the left corner at the edge of the bar was a small table with a picture of Snazzy in his Army uniform. I approached.

Snazzy looked very different from what I remembered. Naturally, his long hair in his older life covered what was at one time quite a baby face as in the photo.

"He was a great, great man," an older gentlemen remarked.

I turned. Standing behind me was an old man wearing jeans and a tucked in long sleeve shirt. The shirt had what looked like Silver Slayers insignia on the shirt pocket.

"Yes," I replied.

The man smiled. "Young man, I don't believe I know you. Prospect?"

"Oh no. I'm Doozy, brother."

We shook hands.

"I'm Quentin. Old friend of Tommy's," he said.

I stared. "Tommy?"

"Sorry, Snazzy. His name was Tommy. Knew him since we were kids. Didn't his old lady come with you guys?"

I had never met his old lady. I shook my head.

"You're new alright. She should be here. Rhonda, or Indie, as they call her."

133

"Doozy what are you doing bothering this fella!" Hacksaw interjected.

Quentin's face lit up. "Hacksaw!"

The two hugged and briefly reminisced.

"Doozy," Hacksaw said, "Do you know Quentin?"

I nodded.

"But do you know who he is?"

Quentin pulled a business card out of his shirt pocket.

"Son, this is my Tavern. Guildy's goes back to my great-great-grandfather. Guildy Giles, he let them boys shack here during the war. Yankees and Rebels. Rebs by choice, those Yanks, well...you know how it went."

"Pleasure to meet you. I've been here a few times before," I said.

He smiled and nodded. "I've seen you, but you were busy."

The last time I was at the tavern I had companionship of the female sort.

"Oh, yes I was," I laughed.

Quentin patted me on the shoulder and walked off. I looked back at Snazzy's picture and the cards and flowers surrounding it. The Navy, let alone the period I served in, had to be much different than what Snazzy experienced in the Army. Beyond the oath taken at enlistment, I suspected that he and I had little in common regarding what we did in our respective fields. He had a Purple Heart. I had more routine ribbons of sea service and good conduct. I reflected for a moment before approaching the bar to get a beer.

"And you, you freakin almost ran into me!" Crud called out.

I looked. "Oh, that was from the damned wind getting under my riding glasses and making my eyes juice up."

Crud, with a beer in hand, playfully slugged me in the stomach. "Don't let it happen again."

I patted him on his back as I walked on to get a drink. The bartender was a cuter, younger woman than the others I had seen before. She had reddish hair with light freckles and green eyes.

"Okay handsome. What'll it be?" she said.

I smiled. "Just a light beer. Gotta stay spry, honey."

"I'd ask ya for ID, but Quentin seems to like you."

She gave me a draught pint and winked.

"Thankya....?"

"I'm Cindy."

"Doozy. It's a pleasure," I said.

Just then, Waltz walked up and put his arm around my shoulder.

"Doozy, you best not be giving Cindy any trouble" he said.

"Nah, I was just telling her it was a pleasure. I'm crazy for freckles."

She tilted her head and smirked. Some Silver Slayers stood at end of the bar tapping their glasses to get her attention.

"I'll be back," I playfully said to her.

Waltz and I began comingling with brothers of Bones and Wheels and Silver Slayers. I knew little of the 'Slayers except that Mutt was the President and the Treasurer, Clapper, was at one time in Bones and Wheels. Nobody explained why he switched over. Waltz chatted with the bunch as I stood sipping my beer.

"Young stud," a woman said.

To my right was an older woman with long white hair and a patch-heavy 'Slayers cut. The name patch read, "Sissykiller."

"Hi," I greeted.

"So you're that new kid. Patched in finally."

"In June."

"I'm Sissykiller. Mutt's old lady. You're a handsome one."

I smiled. "You ain't too bad yourself."

She reached out and grabbed my rear on the left. "You might want to be careful around here."

"I have my eyes on Cindy."

Sissykiller, tall in her own right, looked past me towards the bar.

"She's a pretty thing. Not sure if you could handle it."

I laughed. "Guess I'd be lucky if I got to find out."

We chatted and sipped our drinks. Waltz made rounds to meet everyone that he could. At some point the front door slowly opened and there stood an elderly lady wearing sunglasses. Her Bones and Wheels T-shirt with the name "Indie" stenciled on the upper left made plain who it was. Mutt and Hacksaw jointly approached and shared hugs and kisses with her.

"Everybody listen up!" Hacksaw announced. Some of the brothers continued talking. Quentin whistled loudly from behind the bar. Cindy and I exchanged eye contact.

Hacksaw raised his hand. "Indie is here, time to gather and pay tribute to the great ones, Snazzy and his old lady."

Waltz, Tank, Crud, and myself walked together towards the portrait of Snazzy. Everyone huddled around as Hacksaw and Mutt walked Indie to the small table and gave her a seat facing the rest of us. Once everyone was quiet, Hacksaw began.

"Snazzy was the last of the three founders of Bones and Wheels MC. We were founded with the Blue Ridge Chapter. Snazzy now joins Loops and Raider in immortality. Of the three, Snazzy was the one that gave the most. He was injured in combat in Vietnam, the owner of a local auto service station, a father and loving husband. Today we give his old lady, the last connection to our founders, his cut. We love you Indie, and we are always here for you. Bones and Wheels brotherhood."

Hacksaw handed Snazzy's cut, which I'd never before seen. It was nicely folded and had all the patches and tags anointed to a founder. I felt like I knew Snazzy, but in fact I only knew of him through the members as he had been ill for some time. Just then, Mutt approached Hacksaw and embraced him. He then gave condolences to Indie. She stood.

"Ah he was a sonofabitch," she said.

The brothers looked at each other.

"But he was sexy, he was mine, and damnit I'm 'gon miss him!"

Members of both clubs raised their glasses and voiced support and agreement.

"Alright you bastards!" Mutt started, "Don't drink too much here, we have a show at the club house tonight. Silver Slayers and Bones and Wheels will together honor Snazzy. He was a good man, and we must honor our Vietnam vets! More and more of them pass each year!"

Brothers nodded and voiced agreement. Just then, Sissykiller approached me.

"I hear Cindy will be at the club house later."

I faced her. "Oh yea?"

"She's single."

I looked toward the bar. Brothers were getting their final rounds or paying up. Some started leaving and firing up their rides. Cindy glanced at me and smiled.

"Well," I said to Sissykiller, "Maybe tonight will get interesting."

She nudged my shoulder and walked away smiling. I approached the bar and contemplated getting one more drink. Cindy approached.

"Another one?"

I grinned, then Crud and Waltz intervened.

"No, he's rolling with us. We gotta help set up for the band at the 'Slayers joint," Crud said.

Waltz nodded. "You'll see him if you come out."

She smiled. "I just might. You boys ride safe, ok?"

I paid for the drink and left with Crud and Waltz. A handful of our guys and some 'Slayers had already left. Indie offered anyone a ride (anyone driving a car was driving "cage") who drank too much, but everyone was too proud and boisterous. I cut on my ride, let it purr for a moment, then waited for Crud and Waltz to ready themselves. We were riding as a trio to the 'Slayers club house. It was just north of Washington, a small town not far from Sperryville; certainly not to be confused with the nation's capital.

Blue Ridge Riders Part II

Waltz, Crud, and I proceeded to exit the gravel lot at Guildy's Tavern onto north U.S. 211, Lee Highway. Crud inadvertently rode into an unforgiving pothole when a speeding car forced him to swerve. He put down his Street Glide. I immediately turned back into the gravel lot to park and check on him. Waltz sped off to chase the car as it bolted northbound.

"Crud, damn. You okay?" I asked.

I helped him get his ride up. A few other riders, Bones and Wheels and Silver Slayers alike, hopped on their rides to follow suit with Waltz. Tank ran up behind me.

"What the hell happened?" he asked.

"Dumbass driver. Had to be going 20 over, easily," Crud replied.

"How does she look?"

I saw a ding on his fuel tank's left side. The clutch side of the handlebar looked a bit warped as well.

"Not horrible, but sure as hell not good," I said.

"Got my hand a little. The glove worked out though," Crud added.

Tank shook his head. "Jesus, these people today. If it doesn't have four wheels it doesn't count for them."

140

Hacksaw and Loveflame rode up. "God damnit, what the hell!" Hacksaw barked.

"I'll try 'er out. I think it's good enough to ride," Crud answered.

"You can ride cage with Indie if nothing else!" Loveflame added.

Zany approached Tank, then told us that Quentin had a trailer we could strap Crud's ride to if need be. He offered to keep it in the shop next door until it could get fixed up. Crud opted to try riding as the 'Slayers clubhouse was only a seven mile ride from the tavern. The sun was slowly being swallowed by the Blue Ridge to the west of us, and the air began turning sharp and cold. Hacksaw and Loveflame remained on their ride sitting in neutral as Crud got back on the Street Glide to try it on the highway. The left blinker was out, but Crud nodded and signaled "okay." Hacksaw followed behind. I looked at Zany and Tank and shrugged. Off we were.

Evening was arriving quickly, but the ride from Guildy's Tavern to the 'Slayers clubhouse was a nice one. We stayed on Lee Highway past the junction of U.S. 522 and proceeded northbound. The highway widened into two lanes both ways as we rode in the right lane going a solid 55. Everyone watched Crud who rode in front carefully. I noticed Ironside quickly approaching from behind, and after him Indie driving cage. We turned left onto U.S. 522 Business route through Washington, Virginia. This

Washington was unique in that it was charted by George Washington himself and was an older municipality than the District of Columbia. Cuter and cozier than Sperryville, the town of Washington was a destination of yuppies from Washington, DC. They mainly came on weekends and had retreats in the area because of its beauty and isolation. Rappahannock County itself was free of stoplights. Along with the with locals, we cared little for the yuppy types as they cared little for us. Parked on the streetside were expensive SUVs and hybrid cars, a solid indicator of the urban-suburban types that frequented the area. We received a few stares as we rode through. Neither Waltz nor anyone who rode off chasing the speedster were seen. I didn't get a good look at the car anyway, except to say that it was a light blue SUV of sorts.

We made a left onto State Road 622. It was a very narrow, cute farm road that veered westward towards the Blue Ridge. The sun was now entirely behind the modest peaks and the orange sky turned dark, dark blue. My cheeks began to feel bitten by the crisp cold air. Thankfully, my eyes remained free of tears. Crud was fortunate that his headlight worked, as did his taillight. Our formation tightened up as we weaved left and right on the narrow road towards the Silver Slayers clubhouse.

Following Crud, I wondered if he knew where we were going. He rode slow, and after a few miles we stopped. Hacksaw rode up beside him while

Tank rode up next to me. Ironside and Indie were immediately behind us.

"Don't worry kid! He knows where it is!" Tank said over our rumbling rides.

"I ain't worried. A little curious I guess!"

"That crap pisses me off. Those damned drivers. Probably city folks too."

"Do you think Crud will ride out of here tonight?" I asked.

"Nah, we'll get him liquored up and he can either stay up here or get a ride."

Hacksaw whistled and then signaled for us to proceed. Crud started first, then Hacksaw, then the rest of us. About another mile down the road, we veered right onto a gravel stretch that led to a well-lit barn. It was undoubtedly the 'Slayers clubhouse. I was impressed; the barn was large and through the closed doors the lights were especially bright. A row of cars, trucks, and motorcycles were parked to the right in the grass. Dimly beyond the barn was a large, white antebellum house. We pulled up near the closed barn doors before Crud and Hacksaw rode beyond. Tank signaled for me and Ironside to park with him near the other vehicles. Indie parked further down.

"What the hell happened with Crud?" Ironside asked.

"Dumbass drivers not paying attention. He had to dodge a speeding car," Tank said.

"He could've left the Street Glide with Quentin at the tavern."

Tank chuckled. "You know Crud."

Ironside nodded. Indie approached us.

"Well boys, you can be my entourage into the party!" she said.

"That, would be our pleasure," Tank replied, putting his arm around her.

We proceeded towards the barn.

"So, who's this young man?" Indie asked.

Ironside patted me on the back. "This is Doozy. Our newest brother. Navy guy."

"Doozy, are you single?"

I looked at her. "Something like that."

She pinched me on the side. "You may change your mind."

Vocals and instruments sounded from beyond the doors. We slid the door open to enter. The barn was spacious, with industrial-style vertical lights set up. There were chairs in front of us and to the right a makeshift bar with a beautiful brunette serving up drinks. To the back was a stage where a band was setting up. Above was a loft where a large American flag and a large Silver Slayers MC flag hung. The Silver Slayers colors featured a knight's helmet with glowing eyes and a medieval axe crossing a sword from behind the helmet. There was no chapter sign and asking seemed pointless in the moment.

Everyone cheered when we entered with the star of the party, Indie. Many were present who were not with us at Guildy's. Crud and Hacksaw along with Loveflame entered from the back. Ironside approached them as Tank, Indie and I stood near the front.

"Let's get you a seat," Tank said to Indie.

"Thankya hun," she replied.

I thought about the arrangements for the night and whether people were staying at the barn or house or if we were expected to ride home. Front Royal was a good 20 miles from where we were and that wasn't counting where I actually lived, which was in Marshall. The party was not really on yet, so I chose to start with a drink. The bartender's beauty aided the decision to do so.

"What can I get ya darlin?" she asked.

"Surprise me."

She smiled as she began making a concoction. The ring on her finger implied that messing around was not ideal.

"Nothing fancy," she said, "But the boys like my scotch and soda."

"Works for me."

I retrieved some cash as she handed me the drink.

"Oh no. It's part of the party." she insisted.

I smiled and winked. "Have a few bucks for a tip."

Placing cash on the bar, I proceeded towards the stage to check out the band. There were T-shirts laid out on the stage.

"Rappahannock Reelers?" I asked aloud.

Standing behind the shirts were two men and two women. The man setting up the mic looked.

"Ah ya, we know Mutt. My pops knew Snazzy. Quentin over at Guildy's too. We're honored to play here tonight."

"Cool deal," I replied.

"I'm Tim. The two girls are Sandy and Trish. The guy messing with the drums is Pete."

"I'm Doozy. Pleasure."

We shook hands and the others waved. I followed suit. Just then, rumbling sounded outside, ruckus enough to indicate a good sized group of riders. Everyone looked towards the sliding doors which were now open. A group of brothers and Silver Slayers seated with Indie stood. The light inside poured out into the darkness revealing Waltz's face as he and others rode close. I approached to ask about what transpired with the speeding buffoon. They parked just outside the doors.

"Waltz. We were a little worried man," I said.

He unstrapped his helmet and removed his riding glasses. "Some DC assholes. We got them though. They said they were scared."

Hacksaw approached. "Waltz. You know we love you. That was what any of us would've wanted to do. But gotta be careful."

One of the 'Slayers walked up.

"Oh don't worry, we got their tag info," he said.

"Hey!" Mutt yelled as he approached, "What the hell is going on? What did you do?"

"We caught up with them. Actually they nearly ran themselves off the road over by Ben Venue," Waltz explained.

"They went off the road a bit, then we had a talk," the 'Slayer said.

"I get it. We're with you on nabbing assholes that drive like that. But you gotta be careful. No cops?" Mutt asked.

I looked closely at the Silver Slayer's name patch. It read, "Skeeter."

"Nope. We thought about that afterwards," Skeeter explained, "I don't think they called us in either. They knew what they did was wrong."

A few of the other riders involved, Zany and Vin among them, approached. Everyone laughed and hugged. Waltz bumped his fist into my chest.

"Is Cindy here?" he asked.

"I haven't seen her. On my first drink. What are the sleeping arrangements?"

Mutt interjected, "Nobody is riding out of here sloshed. Understand?"

"I mean I'm fine having one or two of these then rolling out later," I replied.

"Like hell!" Indie added.

We faced her. She walked up to Mutt who put his arm around her.

"I bailed Snazzy out of a few bad nights drinking. Sleep in my damned car, or I can give a ride or whatever," she added.

I nodded. "Yes ma'am."

She smiled and pinched me, again. Waltz put his arm around my shoulder and we proceeded to the bar. He understandably took a liking to the bartender. Unlike me, he had no regard for the ring on her hand and schmoozed away. I got another scotch and soda and made my rounds. The band started playing cover material of the southern rock variety. Loveflame, buzzed and chatty, asked about Cal and how he was doing and what we did together. As he was purely a friend I knew through Waltz, there was little for me to explain.

Sissykiller and Mutt approached, asking about my Navy days. My military time was anything but bland, but it didn't include a Purple Heart like Snazzy's did. I tried to play low key about my military service, but Mutt and Sissykiller rebuked my attempts. New arrivals to the party eventually distracted Sissykiller. In quick order, I realized Cindy had arrived.

"Uh oh kid. Look out," Mutt said laughing.

I looked at him.

"My old lady loves to fix up the young men," he explained.

"Oh…"

Sure enough, Sissykiller ran up and hugged Cindy before pointing in the direction of Mutt and I. With the nice lighting in the barn I got a much better look at Cindy. She wore a blue sweater with woman-friendly jeans and a pair of outdoorsy yet stylish ladies boots. The outfit was perfect for her fair and freckled complexion. There was even a little nervousness on my part. She waved. Mutt nudged me forward.

"Jeez man, the woman just got here," I said.

"Gotta start somewhere," he chuckled.

I quickly looked around at the gathering. There were now a lot of people, some plain and non-affiliated with the MCs, others were conversing like they hadn't seen each other in ages. Snazzy's name was being mentioned a fair amount. Crud became increasingly salty about the incident with his Street Glide as he drank. Without realizing it, I was a bit on edge with Cindy present and the unfair pressure on me from everyone insisting I make a move. At the very least, I could crack up at Waltz continuing his pursuit of the beautiful bartender whose name I didn't know.

"Doozy. Told ya I'd be here."

There stood Cindy. I kindly smirked.

"Hey there. Guildy's bore you away?"

She giggled. "Sure."

"Where around here do you live if you don't mind me asking?"

"Are you familiar with Ben Venue?"

I laughed. "Actually yes. Some of the boys had a run in up there with an asshole driver."

"Like the one that busted my Street Glide?" Crud interrupted.

Cindy smiled waved. "Crud. How are you?"

"The drinks are working good," he started, "better than my damned ride."

"Quentin told me. I didn't see it though."

"Ah. It ain't that bad. I rode it here. Just tedious bullshit. Those damned city drivers," Crud added.

He patted me on the back, "You two enjoy yourselves. Doozy, she's pretty."

Cindy laughed as Crud walked away. I glanced at the party and soaked in the sound of the music. Cindy stood with me for a moment before going to get a drink. I checked her out from afar. She was pretty for sure.

"Indie likes you," Hacksaw said as he approached.

I smiled. "I know that's a big deal."

"Sissykiller does too. You have a thing that draws in the older gals."

"It's called being the youngest sonofabitch in the MC."

Hacksaw heartily laughed and patted me on the back as he proceeded elsewhere. Feeling a bit tired, I took a seat and propped my legs up on a chair in front of me. I listened to the band as it went down the list playing classics of rock. Cindy made rounds talking to the brothers of both MCs and the other random guests. I had a thing for her, but I was also careful with I how I conducted myself. It was never my style to be brutish or to sleaze my way into getting lucky with a woman. In contrast, Waltz was taking only momentary breaks from the bar in between his nonstop flirtation with the bartender. I decided to get up and talk to them.

Waltz shared a joke as I approached the bar. The bartender looked at me. I cleared my throat to get their attention.

"I'll get another one please," I said.

"Hey Diane, this is Doozy," Waltz added.

Diane took my cup and made another drink.

"Your brother on wheels here says that you were in the Navy," she said.

I looked at Waltz, then Diane. "Oh. Yea. That was a few years back."

"You're not from these parts are ya?"

"I'm a West Coast kid. It's a long story," I replied.

Diane was a knockout beauty. The brunette hair with the warm brown eyes, a near perfect complexion and just enough lip gloss was more than enough to tempt the hell out of a man. Making matters worse, she wore a beaded white sweater that gave her the angel-look. I couldn't blame Waltz for being almost entranced. I had no agenda that night, but if I did, I was going to stick with Cindy.

"Anyway," I said, "Diane, thank you for the good drinks."

She fluttered her hand at me as Waltz gave a jealous glare. I returned to the chairs to have a seat and listen to music. The Rappahannock Reelers weren't half-bad. Hacksaw, Loveflame, Mutt, and Sissykiller eventually joined me at the seats and bobbed their heads to the tunes. Quentin and Indie sat behind me. Unsure whether or not they were drunk, I could hear their conversation.

151

"…he never knew as far as I know," Quentin said.

"Mandy knows," Indie replied, "But I never told her. She has a sixth sense or something."

"I know that Nick is his."

"He's a spitting image of his daddy. You were a blonde, Nick has black hair just like Tommy did."

"You were mine first anyway. I just hope Mandy isn't torn over any of this," Quentin added.

"You were the better man. Tommy was the love of my life though. Mandy was always his in his own mind."

"But it's all in the past," Quentin insisted, "What goes around comes around."

There was a sound like that of a hand slapping a thigh.

"Yessir. Just like the old days," Indie said.

"Back to our act after this song, babe."

My head perked up almost by accident. It was apparent that I heard something so juicy that I would be wise to play dumb.

"How about those scotch and sodas, Doozy?" Quentin asked.

I faced them, exaggerating how buzzed I really was.

"Oh man. They're good as hell."

Indie smiled. "Isn't the music great?"

I nodded. "It sure is."

Just then, the band finished the song. Quentin and Indie rose to their feet and approached the stage. Hacksaw stood and whistled loudly getting everyone's attention.

"Everybody, everybody outside and everywhere. Gather!" he shouted.

On the stage, Quentin and Indie shook hands with bandmember Tim. He grabbed the mic.

"Alright folks!" he started, "We're at that point where people are getting drunk and rowdy, and whatever the hell else."

Everyone shouted and raised their cups and glasses.

"A real special thanks to Silver Slayers MC for allowing us to host an event for a very dear man, a beloved friend, brother, rider, and husband. Snazzy!"

There was whistling and shouting.

"Snazzy and Indie here have been friends of mine for over fifty years. They shared a deep love, and a loyalty to each other that few ever get. They had two wonderful children and Snazzy had a successful career running Tommy's Auto Repair for over twenty-five years. He was a veteran of the Vietnam War and a Purple Heart recipient. Lastly, he was the founder of Bones and Wheels MC. Blue Ridge Chapter!"

Brothers hollered at the top of their lungs.

"I'm going to let Indie share a few words. But let's make sure we enjoy this night in Snazzy's honor. Enjoy the drinks and the music. Snazzy, wherever you are, this is all for you. We love and miss you!" Quentin finished.

Everyone yelled and whistled as Indy took the mic. The bandmembers standing behind her applauded.

"Quentin always has the best things to say," she said, "Above all else with Snazzy, through everything we had been through, he was the love of my life. We had our children, and Snazzy had a great life as a veteran, business owner, founder of Bones and Wheels, and as a husband. We dearly miss you."

Everyone hollered again. Indie wiped a few tears from her eyes as she motioned to Tim to take back the mic. As she stepped down from the stage, brothers from both MCs lined up to embrace her. I was at the end. When she got to me I reached in to hug her, she predictably pinched my side. Everyone disbursed. Waltz returned to the bar to keep trying his best with Diane. Crud, Zany, and Tank went outside to smoke. Vin, Belcher, and Razzle exited the barn to try some of the 'Slayers "special hard candy."

Tim gave a shout out to Snazzy and then the band proceeded to play a special song in his honor. It was a good tune. Hacksaw, Loveflame, Mutt, Sissykiller, Quentin, and Indie sat together and enjoyed the performance. It seemed that I was on my own for the time being. After zoning out for a period, a woman called my name. I turned and saw Cindy.

"Did you make your rounds?" I asked.

She smiled. "Oh yea, if you're from these parts you always make sure to say hi to everyone."

I nodded.

"Can I ask you something?" she asked.

"What's up?"

"Are you shy?"

I smirked, maybe blushed a little.

"Not really."

"Diane says you're from the West Coast."

I nodded and sipped my drink.

"You wanna go in the house?" she asked.

Her question almost threw me off, but as a man that didn't play games, I made the decision to say yes. We took our drinks and exited the music filled barn though a side door nearest the home.

"Who's place is this?"

She giggled. "Silver Slayers, duh!"

"Nah, for real."

"It's my uncle's. Charlie. You know him as Mutt."

"I figured. But assumptions are the mother of all—"

Just then, Cindy spun me around and kissed me. I hardly knew this woman, she was pretty for sure, but she had a way of also impressing me. Her lips were great, and her feisty nature upped the ante. Some riders and other guests of the party looked on as we went to the house. Once inside, we ran up the stairway that was straight ahead. At that point she was pulling my arm. She pushed me into one of the rooms at the top of the stairway. Though soft up front, I had an aggressive side, and I was preparing to show her. The room was dark, but a large bed was visible to the right. It wasn't often good practice to make love to someone random in a house that was equally such, but things continued to escalate. Somehow, she was on top.

"West Coast boy better be ready," she said.

"You know it."

I furiously flung off my leather cut, my jacket, and my undershirt. I tried unbuttoning my pants, but she lunged into me and devoured my neck and shoulders. Though painful, the setup was fun. After a moment or two I managed to get up and undress her. Under the sweater was an undershirt followed by a black bra. It was noticeable even in the dark due to her fair skin. I began biting and sucking, eventually getting her spun around so she was under me. Doozy may have been soft up front, but once uncaged, he liked to be in charge. Her eyes lit up and she moaned in excitement. I had her well as much as she had me.

"West Coast boy."

I could hear a giggle and someone getting dressed. I opened my eyes. Cindy stood above smiling as she put her clothes on. There were no bruises or bitemarks on her midsection. I always led with lips. She liked to bite. A mirror wasn't required for me to know she left wounds on me.

"That was nice. If you want to do it again sometime…"

"Definitely unexpected," I replied.

"We should probably get back out to the party. You're not big enough to get a room in this house."

"What do you call this?" I asked.

She grabbed my crotch. "Borrowed time, sweetheart."

I laughed. "Entitlement is a sonofabitch."

She leaned over and kissed me before leaving. After a few moments I started gathering my things. For a second my mind panicked that Cindy may have had me and took my valuables. My cut was at the foot of the bed, jacket wadded up near the wall, shirt was tangled with the bed blankets. My pants were under the bed with the knife still clipped inside the right pocket; wallet and its contents in the other. Victory! From there I got dressed and made my way downstairs. At the foot of the stairway the kitchen was to the right. A few Silver Slayers were there drinking and talking. One raised his glass and grinned. On the left was the dining room. Indie and Quentin sat at the table sipping on what appeared to be coffee.

"You made her happy," Indie said smiling.

Quentin laughed. "Hopefully I get a better performance from her at the tavern tomorrow."

"She's nice," I said.

"Hey buster," Indie replied, "if you're lucky she left you her number."

I chuckled before going outside. The band still played in the barn and there were riders and guests all around, some in the dark conversing

157

around the bikes and the cars. I picked up on the smell of pot and fire smoke.

"Yo!" a voice called out.

It was Zany with a cigar clinched between his teeth.

"What's up?" I asked.

He took a puff. "Some of us are rolling out. Are you good or are you going to stay and party some more?"

"Waltz?"

Zany looked toward the barn. "Nah, he's staying. Hacksaw, his old lady, and probably Crud too. That's it."

I remained silent.

"Oh," Zany continued, "And apparently Tank has his trailer here. He's gonna shack up with one of the gals in the band."

I laughed. "I'll stick around."

We hugged. "Cool deal. Enjoy Sunday routine."

"What's that?" I asked.

He took another puff off his cigar and laughed. "Have a good night bro."

Blue Ridge Riders Part III

I wondered what Zany meant by "Sunday routine." As he walked towards the bikes puffing away on his cigar, I shrugged.

"Love you Doozy!" he yelled.

I raised my hand. "Love you too brother!"

I proceeded towards the barn. Zany and other bikers roared down the gravel stretch as the red taillights of their rides were swallowed into the night. The Rappahannock Reelers were finishing what sounded like their final song; the solo was quite impressive. In the barn Waltz and Diane sat in the chairs and conversed. Things were casual between them. At the sliding doors Hacksaw, Loveflame, Mutt, and Sissykiller were sipping drinks and chatting. Tank stood by the vacant bar and gazed at the band. I grinned at the prospect of him picking up one of the ladies.

"You scared her away?" Mutt called out, looking at me.

Sissykiller approached smiling. "Oh honey she did a number on you huh."

I tried playing it down, but my neck was a mess.

Hacksaw and Loveflame also approached.

"Doozy," Hacksaw chuckled, "gotta wear protection."

Waltz and Diane joined in.

"She was nice. Did she leave?" I said.

"You're a West Coast boy. She always wanted one of those," Diane replied.

Waltz laughed. "Bro! Nice going."

It was getting awkward with all the attention. I told them I planned on staying, then Diane returned to the bar and made drinks.

"What, did you go in the house?" Mutt asked.

I nodded. Sissykiller "wooed" and put her arm around me.

"Did you wreck the bed? The house is for the old people and brass," Hacksaw said.

Everyone stared. I had no answer.

"Oh don't worry. Believe me, much worse has happened in those rooms," Loveflame added.

The band finished up its mega solo and began giving salutes to Snazzy, the party, Bones and Wheels MC, and Silver Slayers MC for hosting the event. Everyone applauded. Others entered the barn to join in.

Tim lifted the mic and stand as a salute. "Alright now Tank, you better take good care of the lovely Sandy up here!"

Everyone raised their cups and glasses. Tank nodded and approached the stage. People whistled, awed, and cheered. He and Sandy, with her dark hair and 5'4 120lb frame, kissed as he carried her off.

"She's so tiny in his arms!" Sissykiller said.

"He's a hunk," Diane added.

Waltz looked at her.

"They could've named him Teddy Bear," I said.

I assumed that Tank and the now captive Sandy were going to have some quality time in his trailer out back. Word was that Trish, the taller more voluptuous bandmember, was the property of 'Slayers Treasurer, Clapper, who I had yet to encounter.

"So Tim and Pete don't get any ladies?" I asked.

"Have you ever played in a band?" Loveflame countered.

Mutt shook his head. "You don't shit where you eat, kid."

Indie and Quentin came to mind.

"Pete is twice divorced. He has a lady interest over in Harrisonburg. Tim is happily married," Hacksaw explained.

Cindy entered the barn and gave me a glancing smile. Her and Diane struck up a conversation near the bar. The band finished packing their equipment when a very large Silver Slayer entered through the side door and approached Trish on stage.

"That must be Clapper?" I asked.

"Oh yea," Mutt answered, "Good fella. Don't mess with him though."

I looked on. "Who would?"

"Shit happens, you know that," Waltz said.

I finished the remainder of my drink.

"Okay, so there is a cabin behind the house at the edge of the lawn," Sissykiller said, "that's where you and Waltz can crash. Nobody still here is riding tonight, okay?"

I assured them I wasn't going anywhere. After Diane and Cindy finished their conversation, everyone got another drink. Diane gave me two to get me "young man drunk" and teased me about Cindy. Tim and Pete approached us and bid farewell for the night.

"Doozy, here's our card. Rappahannock Reelers. We do shows all up and down Shenandoah Valley and northern Virginia," Tim said.

"Northern Virginia as in Fairfax area?" I asked.

He winked. "There's still a few joints up that way that call us."

I shook his and Pete's hand. They said bye to the rest of the group. Mutt indicated that there was a bonfire on the property, backside of the house. The after party was there. We helped Mutt and Hacksaw cleanup the barn space and cut off the large lights. Diane wished everyone a good night and prepared to leave. Once she gathered her jacket and purse she approached me.

"Doozy, it was good to meet you. Cindy is a good woman."

We hugged.

"Uh huh. I'd say the same for you too."

Her eyes lit up, and her smile was amazing. "You must have some balls to roll with these boys, but you seem too cute."

She touched my neck and laughed before leaving through the sliding doors. I remained still for a moment to visually enjoy her.

"Doozy!" Waltz called, "bonfire hoss!"

I shifted my focus and went with him. We walked in the dark past the side of the house towards the orange pulsating glow of the fire. Riders and guests remained spread out, comingling. The night was partly cloudy as evidenced by the splotches of stars visible in the sky. Crud greeted us as we approached the fire. He was the only Bones and Wheels brother present. Waltz and I nodded and acknowledged everyone. There were Silver Slayers with their old ladies and a few random folks, some with chairs. One of the 'Slayers was standing off in the shadows having a strange conversation. My attention drew a response.

"Don't worry about him. Just took some candy," another 'Slayer said.

I faced him. "No worries."

"I'm Deviler."

Waltz knew him and greeted first as he was closer.

"I'm Doozy. Nice party."

"I've seen you before but only on big rides," Deviler said, "first time to Prez's place?"

"Nah. I'm the newest Bones and Wheels brother."

"He patched in quick," Waltz said, "did all the rides and helped a lot. Crazy bastard even rode his Sportster in the snow."

Others looked at us. Deviler nodded.

"Dumb. But aren't we all!" he laughed.

He greeted us again, this time with a bro hug. Crud rambled on about his damaged Street Glide as the rest of us casually mingled. A bag of mushrooms was going around, but I simply passed it on. Later, a bag of green came, as did a makeshift pipe made from a .223 shell casing. The night was going well, so I figured, *what the hell*. Waltz, Crud, and I partook. Few people remained at the fire. Deviler began sharing interesting information as my face began to tingle and my eyes opened wider and wider.

"Y'all know the ropes in these parts right?" Deviler asked.

Crud nodded. Waltz too.

"I try to pick up on the vibe," I said.

"These are good people," Deviler continued, "but there's a reason for the push and pull on the MCs."

Crud nodded. "Waltz, Doozy. You know, don't you?"

"Oh yea. I was born in South Carolina, but I grew up here," Waltz said.

"Doozy doesn't see it does he?" Deviler asked.

"See what? I see bulging stars up there. That was some good stuff," I said

Everyone laughed.

"Nah but for real. I'll keep it simple. Indie and Snazzy hold, or held, these two clubs together," Deviler explained.

Buzzed as hell from liquor and whatever green goodie stuff they gave me, I managed to realize what was going on. Indie, Quentin, and Snazzy. A strange, but navigable trio. Still not sure of the innerworkings, I let Deviler continue.

"The great mystery," he started, "is whether or not Snazzy ever knew."

Crud scoffed. "Man, he had to. Shit, he was horsing off too. That's no secret."

"Hey, hey, it's like this," Waltz said.

We stared.

"It's like this."

We waited. Then he pointed at the sky.

"Indie is the center of all this. They love, or loved her. It's almost like instead of jealousy they decided to form or support separate MCs and then simultaneously keep them interconnected, and harmooooonious."

We laughed.

"Harmooooonious? What the..." Deviler laughed.

Crud laughed harder. "Harmooooonious!!"

I   barked.   Then   repeated, "HARMOOOOOONIOUS"

We kept laughing. Waltz fell to the ground laughing hysterically. The night reached an amazing peak of hilarity. We discussed how to play "dodge Cindy" to avoid wounds or how a seat on one of our rides might alter Diane's perfect ass. Someone brought a case of beer to the fire and we sipped on a few. Deviler vomited while Waltz, Crud, and I zoned into a sluggish and tired state. At some point a Silver Slayer not named Deviler lightly slapped my cheeks and told me to get off the lawn and head to the cabin at the edge of the woods. I did so. That was about it.

I blinked my eyes upon hearing voices in the distance. A musty, maroon blanket was draped over me and daylight shined through a dirt stained window to my right. Snoring sounded from beneath. Peering over the edge of the bed I saw Waltz on a bottom bunk. I coughed and clinched my fists to open and close my hands a few times before making my way outside.

"Look who's up!" Hacksaw yelled.

A large group of Silver Slayers and a few brothers stood around the smoldering bonfire. Crud was working to get it restarted. I raised my hand and smiled to everyone's laughter. Mutt approached.

"Doozy, you were. God damn!" he laughed.

"That was some good stuff," I said.

Indie stood with Sissykiller on the other side of the fire. Both waved and smiled.

My voice was coarse. "Mornin ladies."

"I think we properly broke you in. Welcome to our little paradise," Indie said.

"Still handsome," Sissykiller added, "even when you're hungover."

They hugged me from both sides.

166

"Alright, who's up for some breakfast? Good wood is on the fire. We'll get the grill on this thing and get 'er goin'," Crud said.

We remained around the fire as Crud prepared breakfast with the help of Deviler. Waltz eventually stumbled out of the cabin and the others converged on the fire as we enjoyed a feast under the overcast skies. Hacksaw and Mutt explained to me that prospects never come to the Silver Slayers official parties, which is why it was my first. They both strongly implied that in the South things are done two ways: Hatfield and McCoy style, or through the good old soul of hospitality.

"Indie is Queen," Hacksaw explained.

Mutt nodded in agreement. "She had two men, which all of this derives from. One remains a hang around to us, the other was a legendary founder to you."

"What," Indie butted in, "do you think all women in the South are little helpless 'Belles'?"

I remained silent. Her glare gave way to a smile.

"Don't you worry. I look into your eyes and see that soul. You're a stud," she added.

A definite compliment, especially knowing all that I knew at that point. Everyone remained in high spirits as breakfast was cooked. They served bacon, sausage, eggs, and a weird type of grits that appeared over done but everyone seemed to love, except for me. Mutt and Hacksaw left to get ready for "Sunday routine," something I was very much curious about.

167

I got the impression that it was certainly not a church-related matter. Waltz and I talked about the night before and he told me that Cal was not in the MCs because he wasn't trusted with the truth of how our two MCs worked. He also wasn't hated enough to be subjected to any punishment that Indie or the members would inflict on him if he did.

After nearly everyone ate, Tank and Sandy emerged from the trailer and scavenged for what was left. The two appeared particularly exhausted. I laughed at the thought of Sandy performing twice the night before; once on stage for us and once for Tank personally. Just then, a horn sounded and a green pickup slowly approached from around the house. Some people whistled and hollered. When the pickup was closer, I saw that it was Quentin. He rolled down his window.

"Who's ready for Sunday routine?"

Everyone cheered. I was confused, so I watched on. A few 'Slayers, Deviler and Skeeter among them, ran up to the truck bed and retrieved AR-15's, handguns, and a shotgun or two. I was a lifelong gun owner, but the quantity they had was impressive. It was then that I realized there were large dirt mounds in the far distance which served as obvious backstops for anyone looking to target practice. I started to smile at the prospects of what Sunday routine appeared to be.

"Crud, so the rest of our guys that left don't do Sunday routine?" I asked.

He scoffed, then shook his head. "They do it all the time, but they have lives too. This weekend was about Snazzy, which was about last night. Today is just fun, brother."

"Doozy, you've shot guns and stuff before right?" Sissykiller asked.

"Christ," Indie started, "I told you he's a stud. Plus he's a veteran. You know damn well he has."

"What's the coolest shit you've shot?" Quentin, now out of the pickup, asked.

"Fifty caliber off the ship. The machine gun I got to post up with on pier watch was cool looking. Never got to shoot it though. Just counted waves all damned day."

He nodded. "Alright. Go look at the toy in the truck."

I approached the truck bed and looked over the railing. I was quite impressed.

Quentin chuckled. "You know what that is?"

"An old, badass gun. I'm guessing a military grade fifty caliber?"

Deviler patted my shoulder. "M2 Browning machine gun. Fifty caliber is correct. Not bad."

"This baby is from the World War Two," Indie said.

I glared at it with a smile. There was little doubt that we were about to have serious fun. Just then, Mutt and Hacksaw roared up on two ATVs. Both had wagons containing bulky white containers. I quickly realized what it was.

"Oh damn. Tannerite?" I asked.

Mutt grinned. Hacksaw nodded.

I was surprised. "How'd you get that much?"

"You let us worry about that," Indie said, waving her index finger.

Her response worked for me. Crud and Waltz joined the 'Slayers in checking out the guns and retrieving ammo from the pickup. Nobody explained exactly how they were going to shoot, whether it would be competition or just fun. It didn't really matter. The place was perfect for such an activity. The only potential victims of Sunday routine would be the ears of anyone on Skyline Drive or the Appalachian Trail atop the Blue Ridge. It seemed possible that the noise of the gunfire could rumble up its slopes.

"You know I technically have tinnitus from my days working on flight decks," I said.

Sissykiller opened the passenger door to the pickup and retrieved a bag. She threw a pair of earmuffs my way. I bobbled them but held on.

"Were not stupid," she said.

Her answer was satisfactory.

"The M2 is always last," Hacksaw explained.

Everyone gathered around the near-hoard of weapons and grabbed one. Someone turned up music; classic rock. Indie grabbed an AR-15 which I found notable, but with her being the "Queen," maybe I shouldn't have. With the 30 round clips, I was all about using an AR. After everyone picked a gun, Mutt had us lay them down facing the same direction. He and Quentin rode the ATVs a few

170

hundred yards down to the now very obvious backstop mounds to set the Tannerite. This was absolutely a setup I'd never participated in before. I was almost nervous. Everyone's gleam reassured me, however.

Tank lit a cigar and offered me one. I accepted. I nipped the back off with my teeth and spit the pieces out.

"I have a cutter for that," he laughed.

He handed me a book of matches and I lit up. Waltz explained to Hacksaw why he preferred the shotgun. Apparently he liked to see how fast he could empty a pump action. Ultimately, he enjoyed the M2 above all else and didn't care about the opening of Sunday routine, as he put it.

"What kind of heat do you pack?" Tank asked.

"I have an AR, a forty cal, and an Italian made twenty-two revolver, NATO model."

"Not bad."

"It's a family piece," I explained.

"I'm not shooting," Loveflame said, "I'll see how well you do."

I looked, then smiled as I waved my hips. She laughed.

Mutt and Quentin raced towards the makeshift firing line. Tunes continued blaring. Quentin grabbed a shotgun. Hacksaw took an AR that had his name etched in it.

"That's cute," I joked.

Hacksaw lit a cigar and gave a winking grin. We all donned earmuffs and hearing protection and stepped up side by side forming a line. Quentin told Loveflame to give the instruction. Clearly, this routine was routine. She told us to get on our marks. We did. I eased the barrel down range using my one-eye technique for focus. There was a stiff silence.

"GOD BLESS AMERICA."

Loveflame no sooner spoke when an amazing discharge of collective gunfire flashed and sounded continuously. The copious amounts of Tannerite exploding down range was spectacular. The spectacle was something I had never seen before. I was late firing because nobody told me what the cue was. It was clear that they wanted to make an example out of what Sunday routine was all about. I emptied my 30 rounds quickly but with 5 rounds thundering out amidst the depletion of Tannerite and overall silence as everyone else was done. They hooted and hollered and laughed at my slowness.

"You poor thing, slow on the trigger are ya!?" Crud laughed.

Waltz walked up and smacked my back. "I thought you were a veteran. What the hell was that!"

Everyone continued to laugh. I grew angry.

"Welcome to Sunday routine," Mutt said.

Hacksaw approached. "Gotta mess with the newest brother, that's all. Glad you're here though!"

"Next time!" I replied.

The laughing continued. I smiled. Mutt, Quentin, Develin, and Skeeter set up another round of Tannerite down range for Round Two. I was curious as to how much ammo they had seeing as this was a very costly hobby. Indie gave a predictable glare so I dropped the topic. The AR was still my gun of choice, as I wanted to fire as soon as possible and show everyone my quickness. Loveflame sat out again and everyone but Deviler and another 'Slayer named Tats kept the same weapon. We readied ourselves like before, and I licked my lips with satisfaction that this time as we were drawing I knew I would get them.

"FUCK THE COMMIES."

I grew mad at Loveflame almost immediately after she gave the cue. Unfortunately, it didn't change the fact that the mass of gunfire volleyed at blinking speed into the Tannerite was provided by all except me. The collection of explosions was equally spectacular as the first. This time I was even worse off; I fired seven rounds after everyone had finished. I had yet to strike the Tannerite. I was had, again. The laughter was even more angering this time. As it turned out, whenever a brother of either MC attended their first Sunday routine, the others would come up with a list of words or phrases in advance that everyone participating knew, except for the new brother. We did three more sets. I was slow on all of them thanks to not knowing the cues. By the fourth and fifth I no longer cared. The explosions were awesome as was the hard rock playing in the background.

"If you had a shotgun," I said, "you'd miss before the autos got it!"

Everyone looked.

"You were still slow as hell, newbie," Mutt replied.

Loveflame put her arm around me. "Now, welcome to Sunday routine."

"You were quicker than I was my first time," Waltz said.

I wasn't sure if I believed him, but it was enough to lift my mood. Everyone took a break and gathered around the now-smoldering bonfire. Mutt implied that he had connections that helped with gun repair and maintenance which made Sunday routine feasible. After getting to know these folks, I didn't put it past them. Waltz and I agreed to stay for the M2, but we were going to leave sooner rather than later. The two of us still had a bit of a ride to get home. Everyone recounted the night before and how belligerent I got as I rolled around on the ground speaking gibberish. I could hardly remember.

Some left as the rest of us remained around the bonfire. The weather remained favorable for such a setting. I watched Indie as she interacted with everyone, especially the 'Slayers and my brothers. The setup was very unusual to me. Yet, I understood it more and more. Indie seemed to be the type that only rode as someone's woman on a motorcycle, yet here she was commanding two MCs. More interesting was the fact that of the Bones and

Wheels MC, only Blue Ridge Chapter was allowed to participate in the events at 'Slayers clubhouse. Without asking, I deduced that Snazzy was a shadow founder of Bones and Wheels; that Loops and Raider were official founders known to other chapters. Bones and Wheels MC had chapters in West Virginia as well as one near Manassas. I knew a few of them; their names often slipped my mind though. Some sort of very deep lovers triangle, one which Indie was very much in charge of, existed. That the brothers of Blue Ridge Chapter would let such an outsider as myself patch in with them seemed increasingly curious. Prospecting in was no easy task. In one instance, snow turned what was an easy five mile ride into an ordeal I wished to never go through again. Beyond meeting their requirements, circumstances such as that seemed to win them over.

As I stood alone among the group thinking deeply, I noticed Indie routinely peering towards me giving direct eye contact in between her conversation with others. Something odd was at play, and whether or not I liked it, I was now a part of it. The solution seemed simple enough—tow the line. Everyone else was. My mood lifted and I rejoined the group of brothers and 'Slayers alike. Quentin, Hacksaw, and Mutt soon prepared the M2 and got it mounted in a central location. Skeeter rode the ATV out to set up the last batch of Tannerite on site. Everyone looked at me and then Indie approached.

"After the opening of Sunday routine," she said, pinching me, "the newest brother gets to fire our baby first."

"Cool deal," I replied.

Quentin backed the truck up near the firing line as he, Deviler, and Waltz lugged out crates of .50 caliber ammunition. Hacksaw and Mutt rigged the gun to an M63 ground mount. I unlatched the ammo crate and beheld the beauty of the ammo belt rolled inside. I fed one end of the ammo belt into the M2. Everyone donned their shooting earmuffs. Mutt gave the nod. Sitting on the grass cross legged, I gripped the handles of the sleekly black gun. I scooted my rear on the lawn until comfortable, then aiming as best I could at the Tannerite down at the backstop mounds, I let 'er rip!

The pounding, the violent "glug, glug" sequence of each round firing off, sent my mind into yesteryear. The days onboard the USS Peleliu when we fired the 50 caliber at smoke targets in the South Pacific made me grin. In the present, I was grinning as well. The rattling of the M2 as I fired it threw off my aim and the first shots failed to land on the Tannerite. Within seconds, however, the explosion was complete. Everyone cheered. I ceased firing not long thereafter. I stood as I removed my earmuffs.

"Whooooooo baby!" Waltz patted me.

Indie and Sissykiller hugged me, one on each side.

"Alright Doozy," Indie said, pinching me again, "welcome for the final time. Stay a stud."

"I'm too young for you!" I joked.

Hacksaw laughed. "Boy, nobody's too young for her."

Everyone joked and talked around the fire for a time. Skeeter and Crud rode the ATV's and set up a variety of 20x20 illustration targets from Osama bin Laden to Adolf Hitler to Jeffrey Dahmer. At the distance the targets were, striking them would prove difficult except for rounds sprayed relentlessly in their vicinity as the M2 could beautifully do. Loveflame took the reigns next followed by Waltz. He and I got ready to leave once he finished. Farewells for the day were in order.

"Welcome, brother," Hacksaw said as we hugged.

Mutt bro hugged me. "West Coast out here. You're a strange cat. See ya next time."

"Doozy, ride safe. Wear protection to keep them fangs off your neck too!" Crud joked.

I pat him on the back as we hugged. "Hey man. Yea, but you might need protection from speeding assholes."

He grinned, then Quentin shook my hand.

"Alright kid. You panned out. Blue Ridge Chapter wouldn't have patched you in if you hadn't though. See you around."

"We'll always stop by Guildy's," I replied.

Indie grabbed me from behind. "Don't be distracting Cindy when she's working. Understand? She shoulda gave you her number."

"I never got to say bye to her before she left," I said, laughing, "maybe that was a hint."

Indie pinched me. "You just keep being a stud, love."

Loveflame hugged me next. "You and Hacksaw will probably be riding to Fredericksburg next week. I'll see you at the house for the next meeting. Take care."

I hugged her back. Deviler, Skeeter and the remaining others said bye. Deviler reminded me in the fewest words possible to remember where I was and who I was a part of. I fully understood and was content with it all. With that, Waltz and I proceeded towards the barn to our Road King and Sportster, respectively. As we strapped on our helmets and readied to cut on our rides, I felt compelled to ask him about things that previously slipped my mind.

"How long have you been a part of Bones and Wheels?"

"Three years," he replied.

"I probably should know by now."

Waltz continued. "I came on just before Snazzy fell ill. Other founders were gone before I patched in."

We cut on the bikes. I talked loudly over their rumbling.

"How well do you know these guys?"

"Diane is Mutt and Sissykiller's daughter," he said, "they never said I couldn't try with her, but I'd never dare cross a line."

"Bro, she's married!"

He grinned. "Nope. They got her that rock to protect her. It hardly works though. They won't just let me have her, but they've left the door open if she decides to say yes."

I stared.

"I'm working on it," he finished.

I was blown away. The intertangled social fabric of these particular MCs was beyond my comprehension, and yet they somehow trusted me as a brother. As best I could tell, Indie's continuous reference toward me as a "stud" was the mark of approval. The thought wasn't lost on me. Waltz and I started down the gravel stretch to State Road 622. After meandering our way back to Washington, we stopped side by side at the T intersection waiting for traffic.

"So that makes Cindy and Diane cousins?" I asked.

Waltz nodded. "But Cindy is fair game. The door is open for someone worthy."

We proceeded left onto State Road 628 to Flint Hill and the intersection of U.S. 522. Once more, we stopped side by side while we waited for oncoming traffic.

"I'm surprised she didn't give you her number or anything," Waltz said.

I shrugged. "It's all good. There's lots of fish in the sea."

We proceeded left onto U.S. 522, then right onto State Road 647. The sun slowly approached the peaking horizon of the Blue Ridge, having broken through the overcast skies. The air turned crisp and cool as orange and red leaves continued to flutter off the trees like the previous day. Deer stood precariously on the edge of the road, but thankfully remained in place. The pleasure of weaving on country roads like 647, through foothills and past beautiful quaint homes, made longer distances seem short.

Once at Interstate 66, Waltz slowed down and leaned right accelerating up the on-ramp as he stretched his arm out to signal farewell. I raised mine as I proceeded straight under the overpass onto Route 55 into Marshall. A married couple that traveled constantly had kindly rented a room to me a few months prior. Once home, I changed into gym shorts and a casual T-shirt as I prepared to lounge and watch TV. The edge of a slip of paper became exposed from the left pocket of my leather cut when I threw it on my bed. I retrieved it. Written in ink was "Cindy" followed by a phone number and three hearts.

A Lovely Life

Waking up to existence
Waking up to a bedroom's distinct smell
Waking up to coffee brewing
Waking up to show and tell

A lovely life indeed
Dangers abound to include feelings and sound
Limited time for organs to function
Limited time to see, touch, and feel

A lovely life
Opportunities to do good and bad
Opportunities to learn
Love to give and to take

Life, lovely it is
Death could come any minute
Pondering proves life is current
Accepting reality is fear's only deterrent

Life, lovely life
Challenges give every breath color
Memory gives us fodder to reflect
Opportunity provides means to strive

A lovely life means I am alive

On Sequim Bay

It is a blustery Thursday afternoon in January. An intermittent drizzle synonymous with the winters of Western Washington is ongoing. In Blyn, a onetime logging hamlet turned tribal center for the Jamestown-S'Klallam Tribe, a blue lifted pickup turns into a trailhead parking lot and parks along a rock wall. Signage nearby indicates that the parking lot serves part of the Olympic Discovery Trail. Much of the trail runs along what was once the Milwaukee Road—a railroad that had ceased operations on the Pacific Coast decades earlier.

The pickup door opens, and out steps a man in his mid-thirties wearing a ball cap, flannel shirt, winter jacket, carpenter jeans, and boots. These are typical clothing items for a resident of rural Western Washington. The man dons wireless earphones and begins playing music from his cellphone. A slight gust clips his cheeks as he begins a brisk walk southward. To the left is a tribal library, on the right is a roadway separating the trail from a tribal art center. Restrooms are straight ahead near another parking lot along the trail. As the man walks hastily and begins to zone out into the tunes playing, memories are stirred of his past. He is from the nearby town of Sequim, and on this day he walks a portion of the Olympic Discovery Trail shadowing the old Milwaukee Road as it hugs the shores of Sequim Bay.

Tunes blare and the man stares onward down the trail. U.S. 101 becomes visible to the left as does a large, well-lit, gas station and convenience store called "Longhouse Deli." He cannot help but remember back to when he was a little blonde haired boy and an iconic tavern known as "Dickie Birds" stood in that same location. The tavern featured a blue sign encapsulating a white bird. Various adult stories from years earlier about the establishment from men like his father and grandfather kept the place alive in his memory. Without realizing it, the initial memory of the tavern dragged the man into a deep process of thought about his life.

The trail veered to the right in a more eastward direction running close to the foot of Sequim Bay; a spot known as Littleneck Beach. The foul stench of low tide steered the speed-walking man's thoughts toward a more personal memory of him and his grandfather clam digging at what was once a log dump. Adolescent trees grew along the beach where he remembered a two story structure, large driveway, and pilings containing logs dumped by trucks that were waiting to be milled. Along with the music playing in his ears, he drifted into a deep memory about the days three decades prior when he was all of six or seven years old. He and his grandpa turned left off U.S. 101 into the dirt lot at the foot of the bay and the log dump itself.

"No red tide today?" his boyhood self asks.

"Nah. We wouldn't be here to dig clams if it was," his grandpa replies.

"Why is there red tide?"

"It's part of nature."

His grandpa parks the truck next to other vehicles facing a timbered bluff across from the two-story building. They wore rubber boots and had shovels and buckets in the truck bed.

"Why does the tide smell so bad Grandpa?"

His grandpa smiles. "That's the bacteria eating all the dead stuff left when the water goes out."

"What died?"

"Lots of things," he explains, "there are tiny living things that you can't see called plankton and there is the seaweed. It smells as it decomposes."

The two exit the truck, each with a bucket and shovel. The boy struggles to hold both. As they proceed toward the water, various people greet his grandpa. He is a   well-known man about town. Some know the boy as well, though the boy is confused by this. The men are dressed in rugged clothing, dirt spattered boots, thick slightly-torn jeans and tucked in workwear shirts with suspenders. His grandpa partakes in small talk with some of the men as the two proceed to the shoreline. Impatient, the boy continues toward the water as his grandpa chats.

"The mud is trapping me!" he yells.

"Gotta be quick and stay away from the water," his grandpa replies, "the muck isn't as soft there."

Finishing up with greeting the men, his grandpa continues to the shoreline.

"Okay, so the trick is to look for the holes. Those are usually clams, and they will squirt water as you start digging for them."

The boy is excited and begins sprinting around, to the chagrin of his grandpa.

"They don't dig themselves," he continues, "find some spots where you think they are and start."

The boy struggles with holding up the shovel to begin digging, but once in the muck he jumps on the back of the blade to drive it down. The smell gets worse.

"Grandpa it smells like poop!"

His grandpa grins. "Keep digging. I think you'll find clams there."

The boy muscles the shovel up as best he can. When he plops the mucky contents on the ground a few white ovals appear.

"There ya go. Those are good ones too!" his grandpa says.

"But they look small."

"We don't want the big ones. Those are horse clams."

His grandpa instructs him to put the clams in the bucket and continue digging. He wanders for a moment before finding another patch of holes in the muck. This time, when he begins digging, he notices water squirting up.

"They are spitting at me grandpa!" he says.

His grandpa, shoveling clams into his bucket, laughs. "They sure are. Good job!"

"Do you think I will find one of those giant clams?"

"Horse clam?"

"No, the really big big big one."

"Oh," his grandpa continues laughing, "those are Geoducks. They live out there in the bay. Not up here."

"They are so weird!"

"Yes, they are. Now go on and keep digging for them razor clams. The small oval ones!"

The two eventually finish digging and take the bucketload of clams home where they soak their catch in fresh water before steaming them for dinner. The experience serves as a good memory.

In the present, a new song blares through the man's earphones as he smiles. He is now hiking a portion of the trail that runs on the old grade of what was once Blyn Road, past Littleneck Beach and the since-removed log dump. The trail now runs parallel to U.S. 101 on the left. Moss coats the large maples and the scent of the fir, cedar, and hemlock along the trail keeps the man invigorated. On the right is a beautiful but vacant brick home on property now owned by the U.S. Fish and Wildlife Service. The man becomes entranced by the sharp brickwork of the home. *Another memory stirs in his mind.*

"Babe, I love our new apartment," his wife tells him, as the two lay in bed together.

He faces her and runs his hand through her thick, dark hair. The wall past the foot of the bed is brick, sharp in contrast.

"I love you," he says, gazing into her dark eyes.

"I love you too."

They kiss. The TV is on and one of their favorite shows is playing.

"You know I love this show," he says, "but we've seen this episode like a million times."

"Then recite it!" she jokes.

He begins to speak the lines of the characters just before they sound on TV. She laughs and smacks his chest.

"Bet you can't do it," he says.

"I'm good at reciting my bosses lectures at work," she replies, "the asshole says the same thing over and over and over."

He tells her to have at it. She begins mocking her male boss's voice, giving a lecture. She laughs midway through and loses her train of thought.

"You fail!" he teases her.

They playfully wrestle on the bed. She ends up on top gazing into his green eyes. She leans in as the two hold each other arm in arm. Her face glows with joy, her eyes are big and full of warmth.

"You know," she says, "I always feel safe when I'm with you."

He smiles, then leans upward and kisses her. The two make love.

In the present day, tunes continue playing in the man's earphones as his eyes begin to fill with tears. He is long past the brick house and now entering Sequim Bay State Park. The path meanders through aged timber, mostly fir. A recent storm has taken down some trees and sawdust covers portions of the path where crews had to remove them. He continues on eventually reaching a pedestrian bridge spanning over a creek. As he proceeds across, he looks to the right where a road once was. He remembers the family camp that the road linked up with from the rest of the State Park. It had since been removed and the creek now flowed freely into the bay. He recalled the large culvert that once ran under the since-removed roadway. A grin came over his face as he remembers a time at the family camp when he was punished for playing in the culvert. *Another memory.*

"You are the oldest kid here," his mother scolds, "you know damn well that the others are going to follow you!"

His 11 year old self is being punished by his mother. She made him pick out a tree branch to be used for a bear butt spanking. Earlier, he led the other kids to the culvert under the road. With a flashlight, they crawled its length. It seemed like a cool idea except that the adults were not pleased.

"It's a big culvert though. And nobody got hurt!" he pleads.

His mom swats him on the butt with the branch as he hollers.

"I don't give a shit. You know better! You were told not to go in that culvert. You didn't listen," she explains.

"Last time we were here I went into the culvert with Tommy Vincent and nobody cared!"

"I didn't know about that until afterwards. I warned you then too."

She swats him again. He hollers again.

"Okay okay fine fine. I won't do it anymore!"

"Your brother's pants got torn too! I just bought those for him!"

"Maybe he should've been more careful when he crawled through," he argues.

His mom raises the branch as though to swat him again. He flinches.

"Or maybe you shouldn't have led him into the damned culvert! He looks up to you!"

His father sits at the fire cooking breakfast, smiling and shaking his head. The other kids try not to laugh.

The man's mind returns to the present as he smiles and shakes his head. He continues listening to tunes while proceeding on the path. Now out of the State Park, the path again runs parallel to U.S. 101 and approaches West Sequim Bay Road. After a trestle crossing, an open can of beer is visible, laying at the foot of the path. He picks it up and dumps out its contents. Sober since the previous New Years, *he drifts into another memory, this one fresh on his mind.*

There is a driving snowstorm in southern Maryland where he lives. Well over two feet fell, and he lives alone on three acres. He had stocked up on beer in advance of the storm and was intent on sitting it out. Bored, he shovels snow on his long driveway. Drinking and shoveling, he is barely coherent. He finishes shoveling the last of the snow away from his mailbox at the streetside. By now, he has shed all of his top clothes except for his thermal undershirt. He proceeds to his house with no regard for the clothing laying in the snow.

The TV sounds inside as he stumbles towards the refrigerator to grab another bottle of beer. He grabs two before sitting on the couch in his living room. The game show on the screen does little to soothe him as he stares blankly. After chugging the first beer, he pops the cap off the second bottle. Slumped upright on the couch, he drunkenly drops it. Total disregard has consumed him as he sits gazing upon the puddle swelling atop the hardwood floors. Stepping over the mess, he trudges up the stairs to his bedroom. A few moments pass before he returns to the kitchen wearing nothing but his boxers and boots—his Smith and Wesson 0.40 in hand.

Exiting through the double doors at the edge of the kitchen, he steps out onto his large snow covered deck. He wipes snow off the edge railing and places the gun there. The cold seems not to bother his mostly exposed body as he returns to the kitchen to retrieve a box of beer. Plopping the box on the snow at the foot of the railing, he tears off its top and grabs a bottle. After popping the bottle cap off and flinging it into the snow, he chugs and chugs. He grabs another bottle and repeats. Grabbing the gun, he retrieves a third bottle and proceeds down the steps of the deck into the back yard. A dog barking in the far distance is the only sound noticeable as snow begins falling in the otherwise silent atmosphere. He pulls the slide action back on the gun loading a round in the chamber. Using his teeth, he tears the bottle cap off and chugs the beer.

Burping, then throwing the newly emptied bottle into the trees, he gazes at the winter foliage in the distance. The dog barks again. His memory flashes a series of bad images from his past. An awful argument with his ex-wife stings the most. The stone cold silence and isolation brought on harshly by a global pandemic compounds his already complicated life. He raises the gun in his left hand placing the cold barrel against his temple. Sobbing, his mind races through more ugly memories of his past. Squeezing the trigger very slowly, he remains engulfed in dark thought until a sudden flash occurs. Memories of people he made smile, and of those who had helped him along the way take hold. Thoughts, impulses, and a deep tingling in his gut draw him back to goodness, joy, and hope. He grins, then full-on bawls as the gun falls from his grasp. There is no way for him to pull the trigger all the way. A realization that love still triumphs from within is enough to sustain him.

A couple passing by walking a dog brings the man back to the present day as he paces quickly on the trail towards an upward slope. The man and woman nod to him as he does the same. A loud truck passes in the distance to his left, the timber blocks his sight of the highway. The trail continues its incline as it veers left towards some large wooden median posts. The man has arrived at Whitefeather Way, a road connecting the nearby John Wayne Marina to U.S. 101. A pickup towing a boat passes by. The driver waves as does the man. He trots across the road to the opposite shoulder and walks southward towards the trail on the other side. Just past a reader board and a waste container is a porta potty. Beyond, stands the tall and venerable Johnson Creek Trestle—the highest trestle remaining from the old Milwaukee Road.

The man uses the porta potty, remembering to close the toilet lid as instructed by a sign posted above. He exits and steps out onto the old trestle. Now fashioned with railings and solid flooring for pedestrian traffic, he recounts tales from his father about the days when the trains still rumbled across it. A particular conversation between his nine year old self and his father comes to mind. The two are seated at the kitchen table eating lunch.

"We used to play on that trestle," his father says, "back when it was in use."

"Were there lots of trains crossing?"

His father shakes his head. "Not too many, but they ran on a schedule."

They finish lunch.

"One time a train came while me and some friends were playing on it," his father says.

"But dad, how did you live?"

"There were these scary little platforms that extended off the edges of the trestle deck."

"What are those?"

"They were these little square platforms, and we huddled on one as the train passed by. It was scary. The trestle shook and everything."

"I bet you didn't do that again, did you dad?"

"Sure didn't."

In the present, the man looks at a reader board that explains the history of the trestle. There were small platforms, still present, near its eastern and western terminus. The reader board details that the platforms were originally constructed to hold barrels of water for use in the event of a grease fire on the wooden structure. The man smiles at the thought. The trestle was indeed old, built during the era of steam locomotives when railroad fires were prevalent. He continues back the way he came. After reaching Whitefeather Way and crossing it towards the large wooden median posts he passed by earlier, he sees Sequim Bay through a break in the trees to the east. The water gleams as the sun hits it just right—through a gap in the cloud cover. The man attempts to disregard the majestic scene but the shimmering on the water entrances him. *A memory sweeps him up.* Before he knows it, the near-unbearable glow of the sun clips his eyes as it rises on the eastern horizon of the South Pacific.

Wearing a brown turtleneck with woodland camouflage pants and flight deck boots, he walks alongside men and women dressed similarly. The personnel wear shirts colored brown like his as well as red, white, green, blue, yellow, and purple. He is aboard the USS Pelieliu as they gaze at the flight deck looking for debris—shells, pebbles, nuts and bolts, anything that could be sucked into the jet engines of the helicopters onboard. The routine is called "FOD Walkdown." FOD stands for Foreign Object Damage. A loudspeaker blares the voice of the Chief Warrant Officer in charge of flight deck operations, a person better known as the Flight Boss. To his right also scanning the deck for FOD is his good friend, "B-man." The two appear as brothers from a distance, both wearing brown turtlenecks with the accompanying attire.

"How you feeling after last night bro?" B-man asks.

The young man smiles as he retrieves pebbles from the deck. "Head hurts a little. I think that last shot did me in."

"Glad we got back onboard in time," B-man replies, "they weren't kidding about getting underway quickly."

They were in Guam the night before. The ship set sail early that morning.

"Last time I go with you guys. I just wanted to chill on the beach, not close a damned bar down," the young man says.

B-man laughs. "Come on bro, the ladies were pretty and the beats were good."

The line of men and women passes the first two helicopters midway on the flight deck from the rear of the vessel. B-man scoops up shell fragments from the deck. The Flight Boss loudly reminds everyone to continue looking carefully at the deck for debris. The speakers are loudest near the ship's tower.

"Doesn't sound like Flight Boss is hung over at all," the young man quips.

"Nah bro. That guy is a tank. It would take a keg to get him down."

The young man shakes his head. "Are you ready for this next stretch?"

B-man looks at him. "What, until we get to the P.I.?"

"Yea. I'm sure Manila will be wild," the young man says, "not sure how long we will be sailing to get there though."

"It will make for good recovery time at least," B-man suggests.

Shaking his head, the young man laughs. The line of men and women reach the other end of the flight deck. The sun slowly creeps upward remaining unbearable to gaze upon. The water glows.

"Hopefully chow will be good this morning," the young man says.

B-man stares on. The young man continues, "Seems like my stomach is disagreeable on the first few days underway."

"Seasickness," B-man says.

The young man laughs. "Or just shitty food."

In the present, descending the trail from the elevated portion near Whitefeather Way, the man is approaching West Sequim Bay Road. He laughs at the Navy memory; viewing bodies of water often reminded him of those days. A line of people riding bicycles passes by going the other direction. He waves as they return the gesture. A curiously orange pickup brakes fast to avoid striking him as he crosses the road. The driver seems perplexed as he waves him off. He wonders why the driver was speeding and not paying attention. Once on the other side of the road, he traverses a pedestrian friendly trestle watching the waterflow of the stream traveling below. Rustling in the bushes gives way to a pair of deer prancing downstream away from the trestle and his view. *Memories of deer hunting years earlier stir in his mind.*

The man's fifteen year old self stands alongside his father in tall grass near a stump. Both are wearing orange and holding rifles. His father bears a 300 H&H while he wields a 30x30 Savage. The barrels on both guns face the sky. They are on the north face of Lost Mountain, one of the local foothills. He is happy that his father allowed him to miss a day of class. They hiked a mile or so up a gated road to a place they had luck hunting deer in previous seasons. The sound of branches breaking below on the ridge suggests that a deer or other large game lurks. His father slowly readies his gun, gradually aiming it downward in the direction of the sound.

Gesturing, his father directs him to get comfortable and ready to aim. He slowly nods and faces down range. Beneath them is a clearing riddled with old stumps and brush. 50 yards beyond is the tree line. Somewhere between them and the tree line comes another sound. Nothing live is visible, however. They remain seated with guns facing down range. The low rumbling of a plane above distracts them momentarily. He looks up to see if he can spot it as his father pats him in the arm to get his attention.

"Keep focused," his father whispers.

Nodding again, he returns his vision down range towards the tree line. They wait. A rustling much closer to them gets their attention. They look to their left where the sound originated. The source seems to be something small. Just then, a much louder noise comes from down range where they were originally focused. His father stands, barrel aimed downrange in the sound's direction. He stands as well as his heart pounds. He aims.

"Wait," his father says.

More noises sound down range, small trees wave and the sound of snapping branches and twigs continue. Nothing appears in sight, however.

"Shoot?" he asks.

"Never shoot at what you can't see. Never," his father replies.

"That had to be a deer though."

"Maybe so, but did you see it?"

"No."

"Exactly," his father finishes.

They lower their guns, he is disappointed. His father shakes his head and directs them to hike back towards the road. They attempt to tread quietly through the brush and around the stumps. More sounds give way to the sight of birds flocking in directions away from the two of them. Deer are on the mind, not feathered game.

"I bet it was a deer," he says, "it had to be."

"What if it was a person?" his father asks.

He remains silent.

"If we fired and hit a person," his father explains, "the excuse that we didn't know doesn't fly son."

"I guess."

"A gun doesn't have a safety, except for you." his father says.

"I know."

"You have to know what you are shooting at."

"It sucks though. I know that was a deer."

His father stops and looks at him. "Do you?"

"It had to be. Or a bear or mountain lion."

"Did you see it?"

He shakes his head. They hike until they reach an old roadbed that takes them to the mainline where their truck is parked.

"We'll get one next time. Just because it was probably a deer doesn't mean that it was."

His mind returns to the present where he is passing through the State Park again. A smile on his face indicates his inner peace. He is grateful for the lesson of accountability and integrity that the hunting memory brings. While he saw the deer on the creek beneath the trestle, he knows on that day years earlier with his father, they saw nothing but vegetation. He understands that the joy of catching what you seek is never worth the risk of taking the life of someone whose life you did not intend to take. He whistles to the song playing, drawing looks from people passing by.

Across the bridge span from earlier and up a mild slope towards the parallel stretch along U.S. 101, he enjoys the increasing blueness of the sky as the sun burns away the cloud cover. Squirrels stare vertically from tree trunks as he passes by. A glove sits planted on a median pole separating a portion of the path from a roadway that serves as a stretch of the Olympic Discovery Trail. He waves back at an elderly man exiting a car. For the moment he is devoid of memories as the surrounding environment leaves him feeling content with life. For every bad experience there is the knowledge of the good one that provides counterbalance.

The man walks with a continuing smile. The foliage along with the sound of traveling vehicles on U.S. 101 and the chirping of birds in the forest provides a sense of peace and tranquility to his mind. The natural activities around him ground his psyche and the slowly increasing tenderness in his thighs from the speedy pace at which he walks provides a sense of satisfaction. A flash of sunlight beams through gaps in the trees and seeps into his eyes. *His earlier memory returns—he is back in the snow of Maryland.*

The snowy foliage enveloping his property is beautiful, even as the tears continue. The cold remains unnoticeable to his mostly exposed body. He looks up as the flakes of snow lightly fluttering downward contact his face. The cold, melting flakes stream down his cheeks. Laughter takes over as he drops his pistol in the snow. Looking around at his property, he sees the nice pole barn garage, the leafless timber, and behind him the house he bought a year and a half prior. Though his expectations were mostly unmet, the story of how he left his hometown nearly two decades prior and how it culminated in a home purchased on the opposite coast fascinates him. He revels in the memories that led him to where he currently stands; his smile grows. Picking up the gun and the box of beer in the snow, he high steps back inside.

On the trail along Sequim Bay, the man shakes his head and laughs. His antics on that day back in Maryland were not funny in the least bit, but that he reached a point where he acted on such a dark impulse compels him to currently laugh at the oddity that is life. Uncertain at what the future holds, or what his true purpose is, he savors the memories good and bad for what they are—a colorful story of how a man traverses time and age. On his left, the brick house becomes visible again. The path dips down and up, veering left onto the old Blyn Road like before. A person jogs past him waving. He waves back. A motorcycle roars by on U.S. 101 above. The man is impressed by the riders out and about on such a cold, dreary day. *His memory wanders into his motorcycle days.*

The man is cruising U.S. 29 through Culpeper County, Virginia, better known in those parts as "Lee Highway." He is enjoying his Harley Davidson Sportster 1200 with its royal blue and white trim fuel tank. Riding aggressively, he weaves in between cars while holding fast through the dips, twists, and turns going southbound towards Charlottesville. The green summer backdrop along the foot of the Blue Ridge Mountains is distinct. The air is thick and muggy, the smell of honeysuckle serves notice of the part of the country being traversed. He rumbles past a produce truck and makes a quick turn onto U.S. 33 in Ruckersville. Two miles down the way is a roadhouse on the left. He rolls into the parking lot to meet some brothers of his MC.

Standing outside the front entrance to the roadhouse stands the President and Sergeant at Arms of the MC. They embrace, then enter and seat themselves at the bar. He orders a pint of pilsner as the President and Sergeant at Arms order whiskey.

"Good to have you with Bones and Wheels," the President says.

"West coast guy in the brotherhood," the Sergeant at Arms adds, "we got flavor in our ranks now."

He raises his glass to them both. They begin conversing about motorcycle maintenance, women, and an upcoming ride with some other MCs in honor of a fallen club founder. He zones out into thoughts about an ex-girlfriend that used to ride with him everywhere. The feeling of her breasts against his back, her crotch riding up on his rear on the seat, and the reflection in the mirrors of her pink glitter helmet and dark hair waving every which way on a ride anywhere captivates him. A smile appears on his face. The President and Sergeant at Arms take notice and tease him for not paying attention to their conversation. He comes to, lying about what came over his mind. The three continue to drink and chat.

In the present, Littleneck Beach is now to the man's left. On his right is a field with overgrown shrubs partially concealing the visibility of Seven Cedars Casino beyond U.S. 101. He remembers the trailer park that once existed in the overgrown, now-vacant space. The path steers off the roadbed towards the highway. Impulsively, he looks back towards the old road, remembering the times he and his grandpa left the old log dump. His grandpa drove them in his old rusting pickup, white in color otherwise. He remembers the tunes that his grandpa used to whistle. The melodies were unfamiliar to him but enjoyable nonetheless. The man's smile is maintained by the memory.

The trail crosses Jimmycomelately Creek and turns sharply left at the foot of some homes on the shores of Sequim Bay. He proceeds onto the last remaining stretch of old Blyn Road in motorized use and gazes north at the bay in its totality. From the telephone poles lining the grassy intertidal flats to the bay's low rippling waves, he takes in the shimmering sight of sunshine as it beams down on the water. Homes dot the shores on the bay's east and west banks. In the distance he sees a cluster of white poles signifying the masts of vessels moored at John Wayne Marina. He recalls that his father once lived in a home at the very location of where the marina exists today; Pitship Point.

A gust picks up as the man crosses an access road connecting old Blyn Road to U.S. 101. He trots across waving at an approaching motorist in a large pickup. The path follows parallel to the road and passes restrooms and shops belonging to the S'Klallam. More cars are parked outside the shops than when he embarked on his walk. A person with pink hair waves promiscuously at him from beside a car with a rainbow sticker on its side window. He waves back while passing by. Clouds tuck the sun away once more and the resulting dimness makes the gusting air nip his cheeks. He arrives at his truck.

After taking the drivers seat, he pauses. The truck faces old Blyn Road. Beyond that are trees and then Sequim Bay.

"Grandpa," his boyhood self says, "why is there a high and low tide?"

The two are riding home. His grandpa looks and smiles before explaining how the moon plays a role in the phenomenon. In the present, the man leaves the trail parking lot and heads home, smiling.

Farewells and Farts

This one's wrapped up
A book full of literary parts
Better than screams and jeers
Better than thieving kids stealing shopping
carts

Stay tuned
Be glued
Cheer the rude
Dress better than an ex, a prude

There's no better than a bag
Goodies, it is full of
Enjoyable for all; kids and adults, a bum and
hag
The name in reverse – Goodies O' Bag

Previous pages mentioned smoke and drink
Remember "Prissy" the teen who liked pink
And trucks drilling drifters in a blink
Some stories have happy endings – others just
stink

A book is like a life
Beginning and end, there can be strife

Whether it's horrible writing or plots that cut like a knife
Not every line or stanza can finish in a rhyme, so HA

Again, this one's wrapped up
Again, it's a book full of literary parts
And again, better than screams and jeers
Can you guess this last line? Gotcha! It's just *Farewells and Farts*